touchpoint

SHAY LACY, author of *Hero Needed*

CRIMSON
ROMANCE
F+W Media, Inc.

Published by
Crimson Romance
an imprint of F+W Media, Inc.
10151 Carver Road, Suite 200
Blue Ash, Ohio 45242

www.crimsonromance.com

Dedication

To my daughter, Monica, with love. I'm proud of you.

To those who struggle every day to meet the challenges of bipolar disorder, you have my admiration.

To Jennifer Lawler, with gratitude, for giving this story a chance.

As always, to the B-I-C group and my fellow Panera Prison inmates, who hold me accountable. And to my husband, who encourages me to do what I love.

Acknowledgments

To Bill Steele, of HIRE archi in northwest Ohio (*www.hirearchi. com*) who generously shared his knowledge about his profession. Any mistakes are mine, not his.

CHAPTER 1

The building looked like it had suffered a terrorist attack, only it hadn't. Christian Ziko, standing in front of it, looked like any other man, but he wasn't. He was the architect of this destruction and Gabrielle Healey was going to prove it.

The Densmore Building had been a dazzling jewel in the crown of Detroit's revitalized downtown waterfront. The glass third floor jutting out into the atrium with no visible means of support was an impressive engineering marvel. That floor was chosen for the hottest new disco in town.

It became a deathtrap when part of it collapsed, shattering the glass walls and hurling unsuspecting dancers over the edge. Six people were killed and a dozen others injured.

Gabrielle hadn't expected to see Ziko here, since he'd disappeared shortly after the collapse. She thought he might be ashamed or afraid to show his face in public. He should be. With his black hair and dressed all in black, he looked like the cold-blooded killer some thought him to be. Before the Densmore, he'd been touted as a brilliant and innovative architect for his radical designs. Now one local newspaper called him "the architect of death." She wanted to hate him. How dare he create a design so flawed it didn't hold up for six months after it was built?

But she couldn't allow herself to become emotionally involved in her investigation. Her job wasn't to pass judgment, but to gather facts to protect her employer, Michigan Casualty, that had insured the building, from having to pay a claim. Her team had ruled out everything but the architect's design. All she needed was proof to condemn Ziko.

She had so many questions to ask him, and here was the perfect opportunity.

Stepping from the shadows of the building, her sneaker sent a stone skittering across the pavement, announcing her to Ziko. When he turned to face her, she sucked in her breath at what she saw. Lines of strain bracketed his tight mouth and a deep furrow beetled his black brows. But what struck her like a blow was the pain in his Caribbean blue eyes. She almost cried out just looking into their tortured depths.

She'd expected to find a cold, heartless bastard, but tearing pain didn't make any sense. He'd made one public apology…and then remained glaringly silent. He hadn't faced the grieving families, or visited the injured in the hospital, or been on-site during the investigation.

Gabrielle had to touch him. Her clairvoyance allowed her to glean information about a person or object through physical contact. It helped her perform her job as an insurance investigator exceptionally well. But Ziko made her uneasy. There was a darkness about him that had nothing to do with his black jeans and T-shirt. His tee clung to muscled biceps and a firm chest. Her feminine instincts sat up and howled their notice.

She shook off her fanciful thoughts and the unwanted attraction. She was here to do a job, and Christian Ziko could provide the truth.

Taking a cleansing breath, she held out her hand as she moved toward him. "Mr. Ziko? I'm Gabrielle Healey from Michigan Casualty."

At the first touch of his surprisingly cool skin, a picture formed in Gabrielle's mind, clear in the center but fuzzy around the edges. *Christian Ziko sat hunched over his drawing board, his pencil meticulously detailing on the paper tacked to it. It was a drawing of the Densmore and his blue eyes were soft with what could only be described as love as he worked on it. There was joy in his movements, in the light way he held his pencil, and in his bare toes gripping the bottom rung of his wooden stool.*

Gabrielle tore herself away from Ziko and the vision disappeared. She felt shaken by a kernel of doubt. He'd loved it? Then how could he have designed it so poorly?

"Do I know you?" he asked.

"No. Michigan Casualty insured the building. I'm investigating the collapse."

His face closed up and his lips flatlined. "Oh. Well, I'm glad there's insurance money to make repairs."

"Unless they have to tear the building down. The building inspectors have to decide if the Densmore is structurally sound. But I'm not telling you anything you don't already know."

But she was. She could see it as the color leeched from his face, leaving the lines of strain etched starkly into his skin. What the hell?

"I wasn't aware of that," he said.

Where had he been that he hadn't kept up with the TV, newspaper, and radio coverage? "Have you been out of town?" That would explain his absence from the public eye.

He studied the derelict building, his jaw muscles bunching, for so long she thought he didn't intend to answer. Finally one word came out, although reluctantly. "Yes." It was a word full of anger and some other dark emotion. Tension resonated from him. Wherever he'd been, it hadn't relaxed him.

Gabrielle wanted to touch him again to get a picture of what he'd been doing during that time, but she didn't want any more doubts.

Oddly enough, the word that described his present state was vulnerable, as though he was affected by what had happened. But that was crazy. Ziko's lack of public response showed his unconcern.

"I won't keep you from your work." He made a half turn away from her.

"Wait. Let me give you my card in case you need to contact me." She dug in her purse.

"I won't need to—"

"Here," she interrupted, thrusting a card at him. For some reason, it seemed imperative he have a way to contact her.

His hand brushed hers as he took the card and another vision blasted to life in her mind. *A cop slammed Ziko face first against a painted wall. As Ziko tried to rear back, the policeman jammed his billy club against Ziko's neck.*

"I'm innocent!" The wall muffled his shout.

"Tell it to the judge," the cop growled.

Another policeman moved behind Ziko and roughly cuffed him.

Gabrielle jerked back from him, unable to deal with the tumult of emotions the vision caused. This was a precognitive vision, more rare for her. It showed one possible future, if nothing changed between now and then. She was sure she had something to do with this future coming true, but whether it was due to action or inaction, she didn't know.

Ziko headed toward the front door of the Densmore.

"Did your building collapse because of something you did, or was it an accident?" She aimed the words at his back.

*

Christian flinched. Since the press had already slandered his name and reputation, he'd expected her question, but it hurt to hear her accusation. He didn't think he would get used to strangers hating him for something he'd supposedly done, and for some reason it felt worse coming from her.

He turned, the denial automatic. "No."

Then guilt swamped him. Maybe it was his fault. If he hadn't been working on half a dozen projects at once, he would have caught whatever error created this disaster. He cursed himself for not being on-site during construction. Doubt crept in and gnawed at his gut. How could something he'd designed fail?

When he added, "It couldn't have been my fault," even he heard the uncertainty in his voice.

Gabrielle frowned, her gently arched black brows pulling together. "You don't sound certain."

Christian's fists clenched at his side. "Something terrible happened to this building, Ms. Healey. I don't know what, but I couldn't have done it. I build things, beautiful things. I don't destroy them."

"Some of the news reports said your arrogance killed those people, that you were too brash in your assurances the design would work."

There was something he was certain of. "DesignCorp tested my design. Mr. Densmore insisted on it because it was so radical. It withstood all their structural tests."

"Maybe it only worked in the lab."

Stung, he lifted his chin. "No, it should have held up."

She waved toward the building. "Clearly it didn't. A man whose sister died when she fell from the third floor wants you tried for murder."

Someone else hated him. "I didn't know that."

Gabrielle's blue eyes narrowed. "Hasn't anyone kept you up-to-date, forwarded you the news?"

"No." News upset the residents at the Crittenden facility, so medical management blocked it. And his brother Paul hadn't told him any of it, although Christian had been too drugged to care if Paul had.

How had everything gone so wrong that he was considered a worse person in this town than Osama bin Laden? He'd believed the newspapers and magazines when they'd called him the Golden Boy of Architecture. His head had swelled with their praise over his work. Now he was accused of murder. No one seemed interested in proving his innocence, only in exhorting his guilt. Even this woman, who, in her capacity as an investigator, had the power to destroy him.

Gabrielle Healey was a striking woman. Her straight black hair and high cheekbones hinted at a Native American heritage. Her wide-spaced blue eyes were full of intelligence and incisive questions that might probe too deeply. Yet her full lips offered a sensuality he wanted to explore. She was a dangerous combination. She was an investigator and he had things to hide. Things like Crittenden and the reason he'd gone there.

If only she was on his side, she could use that intense mental focus to help him find out what went wrong with the Densmore and prove to everyone's satisfaction he wasn't at fault. Clearly, if he wanted to prove his innocence, he'd have to do his own investigation. He owed it to the dead and to himself to find out.

Gabrielle interrupted his thoughts. "I'd like to ask you some questions."

"I really don't have time." He was afraid what she'd ask, what he might admit accidentally, and what she'd read into anything he said.

She pounced anyway. "Do you have something to hide?"

Yes, he wanted to shout, a mental illness. But he couldn't do that because bipolar disorder had a negative stigma attached to it. It was feared and scorned and misunderstood. And since he'd been at Crittenden, he couldn't afford for anyone to find out, because if they did, they'd blame the Densmore's collapse on it. Just like this woman would.

Instead, he said, "I don't see how I can help you with your investigation."

"Who better than the architect? What can it hurt to walk through the wreckage with me?"

That was a loaded question. Walking through it the first time had caused horrific nightmares and his spiral into a depression that got him committed to Crittenden. He'd been released only a few hours ago and had no intention of going back. He should avoid a repeat performance by steering clear of the interior.

Then why the hell was he here? If he was going to take on the task of clearing his name, he had to go inside. By now, the chalk outlines were probably gone. He hoped the bloodstains had been cleaned up.

"Yeah, let's go inside." He hoped she couldn't hear the trepidation in his voice caused by his belly quivering with nerves.

Gabrielle stopped at the entrance and unlocked the padlock that held the doors chained shut. Christian hadn't even noticed the chain. He couldn't have gotten inside if he'd wanted to.

The interior was dim with so many windows boarded up. It smelled of dust and disuse…and death. Lights high up in the ceiling and along the brick walls came on, lighting his personal nightmare. Steel girders still hung exposed from the third floor structure, looking like at any moment they'd tear loose and catapult into the remaining unbroken panes of glass. One girder lay across the lobby floor like a huge forgotten piece of erector set. Part of the glass ceiling had been replaced by plywood.

This building had been his vision from the moment he first heard Charles Densmore speak about creating a tribute to his late wife. Christian had slaved over draft after draft trying to create a masterpiece of air and light, and he'd thought he had. Somehow his dream had turned into a nightmare. What was left was dreary ruin, the death of his dream.

"Mr. Ziko?"

Christian had a feeling Gabrielle had called his name more than once, but he hadn't heard her. "What?"

"Are you all right?"

"I'm fine." It was a lie, but at least his voice was steady when he said it.

"What do you see?"

"The same thing you do—devastating destruction. This place was beautiful when it was completed." He remembered entering the Densmore for the grand opening. The guests had been awed by the seemingly unsupported third floor overhang. It had been a glittering spectacle that night. Now it more closely resembled a derelict from the ghettos of Detroit.

"Sometimes beauty masks something darker," she said.

"No. I designed it in Mrs. Densmore's memory. She wouldn't have wanted this." A sweep of his hand indicated the current state.

"You're human. You made a mistake."

He looked into her inquisitive blue eyes. She wanted answers, but was there judgment under the intelligent probe? He didn't know. "I thought a man was innocent until proven guilty."

She stiffened and he felt guilty because he'd lashed out.

"So you're alleging you're innocent?"

"It doesn't matter what I say if you've already made up your mind." But it did matter, a lot more than it should have.

"Believe it or not, I'm looking for the truth. However, I do know what the prevailing opinion is."

If only he could sway this one person…but "if onlys" were for dreamers. If only he could go back in time and be on-site during construction, he'd prevent this whole calamity. He looked away from her intriguing face to the wreckage, from one torment to another.

This was his responsibility. He'd designed the Densmore. On paper, he was intimately familiar with every nook and cranny of the building. He was the best hope of finding out why it failed. And if he found he was at fault…well, he'd cross that bridge when he came to it.

CHAPTER 2

Christian Ziko vibrated with a tension that was almost frightening. Gabrielle kept tabs on his whereabouts, not letting him get behind her because she didn't want to be caught unawares in the explosion if he lost it. His face was too pale, his eyes too wide and his right hand made a fist at his side where his arm was stiffly extended. The man had serious issues with what he saw.

"What's your take on the damage you see?" Maybe she could get him to focus away from the internal.

"It shouldn't have happened."

"I know that. I think everyone around Detroit knows that. What's your guess on what failed?"

He pointed at the drooping girders. "Those shouldn't have given way. My design balanced the weight. Those look like the weight was too much."

His gaze moved to the girder in the middle of the atrium floor. "Too much force on the outer edge. But it's just not possible."

"Obviously it is."

"I need a failure analysis of the support beams to determine what stress loads they experienced."

"The building inspector did one. So did Michigan Casualty." She wished she'd brought her copy with her. But he'd find out the results after the grand jury was through looking at it. Did he knew about that aspect of the investigation, since he was unaware of everything else? As volatile as he was now, she didn't want to be the one to tell him.

"Without the failure analysis, what can you tell me?" she asked.

"The breakdown began there." He pointed to the third floor where the support beam was missing. What was left of the floor sagged toward that point. "Instead of the force being distributed to the beams imbedded in the outer walls, as I designed it, it looks like it spread to the floor edge." A frown pinched his brows together. "That's not possible."

"It's possible. After all, the overhang was unsupported."

Ziko shook his head. "It only appeared to be unsupported."

"As you can see, the beams failed to hold the weight."

The look on his face was like a trapped animal's—too much white in the eyes, too many strain lines. He dragged a hand through his already disordered hair, mussing it further.

"It can't be." He said it as though to himself, then added, "A supplier must have substituted on the materials."

"We checked. Each supplier provided exactly what was specified on the materials order."

"Then there was a typo on the order."

"No. We double-checked the orders to the drawings. They match."

His chin came up. "The drawings were flawless. I double- and triple-checked them before submitting them."

"If we ruled out everything else, it has to be your design."

He pinned her with his gaze. "Did you rule out everything else?"

"Yes."

A look of agony passed over his face. He walked further into the atrium until his back was to her. Glass crunched under his white sneakers. She tried not to feel pity toward him as he stood framed against the backdrop of his shattered dream. He should have done more extensive testing, and then this disaster wouldn't have happened. Perhaps it was a cost-cutting measure not to do additional tests. Or maybe it was greed.

From what she'd seen in the past few minutes, she didn't think he was motivated strictly by money. But she was a poor judge of character. Men she'd thought she could trust and respect, men who'd seemed grounded in reality had all turned tail and run when she told them she was psychic. She was the last person who could say anything for certain about other people, even if she was touching them. She just wasn't reliable.

The facts suggested Christian Ziko's design was flawed. The facts suggested his design had resulted in the deaths of six people.

As though she'd spoken out loud, Ziko reacted to her thoughts. "I need to see the results of the investigation."

It would be a serious conflict of interest if their main suspect sifted through the evidence. Although if he was brought to trial, his attorney would get to see it all anyway. But it wouldn't be her that leaked the facts.

"I'm afraid I can't help you."

"What?" When he turned toward her, he looked confused.

"I'm sorry. I thought you were talking to me."

"No. Who do I talk to about getting a key to this place?"

"Mr. Ziko, I don't think anyone will give you a key. Not yet, anyway."

He frowned. "Why not? What do you mean?"

"You're under suspicion, you must realize that. No one would want to give you the opportunity to tamper with evidence."

There was an instant of extreme vulnerability in his face before grim resolve tightened his jaw. "You let me in."

Oh shit. Her action was going to come back to bite her in the butt. "I wanted your take on the destruction."

"You wanted me to confess."

Gabrielle's conscience hurt for a moment until she remembered the dead. "Yes. I want to know what happened."

"At least you're honest. How long do you intend to be here?"

"Not long." Just enough time to touch the building again and see if she got a different reading from it than she had all the other times she'd touched it in the past two weeks.

"Oh. Then, if you don't mind, I'll let you do whatever you came for while I look around."

"The building's not safe inside."

His blue gaze blasted right through her. "Do you care if I become another casualty? In your mind, wouldn't that be a fitting end for me?"

Before she'd met him, that would have been her opinion. But his vulnerability gnawed at her. He wasn't what she'd expected.

So her answer was a little evasive. "I think the families of the victims want a different kind of closure. They might want you dead, but they want you to suffer like they are."

Her words were a direct hit. Pain flashed across his face. He turned away and walked toward the interior of the building. Remorse tore through her. She'd never been intentionally cruel before. Not that she'd meant to hurt him—she'd just wanted a reaction out of him. Too bad his reactions kept surprising her.

Before she could stop him, he opened the door to the stairwell.

"Wait!" she shouted. "You can't go up there."

His blue eyes blazed with defiance. The last glimpse she had of him was his shoulders thrown back and his chin lifted as he disappeared through the door. There was the arrogant architect the trade magazines wrote about.

Gabrielle ran after him. If he was suicidal, she couldn't let him kill himself on her watch. No, she wouldn't be responsible for that.

Flinging open the door to the stairwell, she found only emptiness. My God, he was fast. She jogged up the stairs, thankful for daily workouts on her treadmill. At the second floor landing, she heard a footstep on the stairs above her.

"Stop, Mr. Ziko! Don't go up there."

When she got no response, she continued climbing. Her thighs burned from taking the stairs too fast. Before she reached the turn, the third floor stairwell door slammed.

Damn. She'd never catch him. She didn't want to see one more body splattered in the atrium, his limbs twisted into unnatural contortions.

She double-timed it up the rest of the stairs, reaching the door out of breath. As she jerked it open, she realized she didn't know what direction the atrium was. Damn, and Ziko did because he'd drawn the floor plan.

Think, Gaby. The disco owners had taken down all the signs for the dance club. She tried to place her current location in relation to the lobby below. Right. Go right.

She ran to the end of the short corridor and turned the corner. There were the glass doors to the disco, but no sign of Ziko.

Sprinting the short distance to the doors, she swung through them and skidded to a stop. Fifty yards ahead, Ziko stood precariously close to the tilted edge. She sucked in her breath and tried to prepare herself for the sight of him throwing himself from the rim.

"Ziko, don't do it!"

He didn't turn or indicate in any way he'd heard her. Then he moved forward and she flinched. But he only squatted down and ran his palm over the floor.

She frowned. What was he doing?

Moving cautiously forward, her curiosity awakened with a vengeance. She hadn't been up here. When the building inspectors couldn't confirm the safety of this floor, Michigan Casualty had paid experts to do an evaluation. They'd done so with safety ropes and harnesses, all the equipment to save them from a nasty fall.

But Ziko had none of that. He was on his knees now, moving left to right as he studied who knew what. Gabrielle stepped closer. She couldn't shake a sense of uneasiness, or the icy finger tracing her spine. She wanted to clutch at the support beams, but she didn't know how secure they were. Ziko was too close now to the jagged hole in the floor.

"Don't get so close." She was careful not to yell and startle him, lest he fall and she be directly responsible for his death.

An ominous groan from the floor went right through her like an electric current and she stiffened. "Get back from the edge!"

Amazingly enough, Ziko obeyed, giving the depression in the floor a wide berth. Her heart was in her throat and she did clutch the vertical support.

A vision blasted into her mind with the force of a speeding train. *Young people dressed to party ran past where she stood, the women screaming in terror. The floor shook as though in an earthquake. Beyond the fleeing bodies, she saw a sandy-haired young man pinwheeling his arms, and then he tumbled backward over the crumbling edge with a cry. The most awful sound competed with the screams, a screech like when a nail was torn from a board, only much lower pitched and slower, a haunting sound, as much internal as it was external. Gabrielle heard the shattering glass and knew the support beam had torn loose and struck the atrium floor with the force of a bomb. Screams rent the air. The cacophony of sound was deafening.*

"Miss Healey? Gabrielle?"

It was physically wrenching to tear loose from the past, but Ziko's voice finally broke through the horror of the floor's collapse. He stood less than a foot away from her, not touching, but invading her space all the same. His blue eyes showed concern and something else she couldn't decipher.

"What?" Her voice sounded hoarse and choked to her ears.

"You shouldn't be up here if you're so afraid." His hand opened and closed by his side.

She took a small step to the side without trying to look like she was moving farther from him. But she didn't want him to touch her, not right now. "I didn't get to investigate this floor myself. I want to."

"You know it's not safe."

"You're here."

"I have to know why it isn't safe. If you'll go back downstairs, I'll be down in a few minutes."

"I'll wait for you here." She crossed her arms across her chest to prevent further argument. She had her own probing to do, and if he'd turn his back, she'd do it.

He stalked back toward the edge, although his steps became gentler the closer he came to what had been a glass wall. He bypassed the depression in the floor and hunkered down nearby to once again study the floor.

Moving farther away from the center of the collapse, Gabrielle found a position out of Ziko's line of sight and dropped to a crouch, gently laying a hand on the floor. She wanted to see the building being built, the decisions that had gone into this floor.

Softly a scene began, blurry but coming into focus. *A man in a white hard-hat holding rolled up drawings stared out at the exposed beams of a building not yet finished. She knew from his photo this was Ziko's partner, Roger Barrett, a successful architect in his own right, but of the traditional sort. His designs were timeless, not groundbreaking like Ziko's. His light blue eyes were possessive as he viewed his creation, but they didn't hold the love she'd seen in Ziko's eyes.*

She didn't care about Barrett's involvement in the building. She wanted to see Christian Ziko. She shook away Barrett's image, but try as she might, no image of Ziko appeared. She didn't understand it. Why couldn't she picture him on this floor?

"What are you doing?" Ziko's voice snapped her out of her musings.

Her temples throbbed from trying to exert control over her vision. She tried to think of a plausible answer quickly as she rose to her feet. "I was duplicating your movements, trying to see what you saw." Boy, did that sound stupid.

"You're not an architect."

No, she'd had to give up that dream and had ended up at the other end of the spectrum, after buildings were destroyed. "I have enough knowledge of how buildings are made to make educated guesses."

Ziko looked like he wanted to probe further, but then he glanced away. "Do you have measuring tools with you?"

The question startled her. "No, not today."

"Too bad." He strode away from her, his long legs carrying him to the edge in moments.

He went so close to the drop-off Gabrielle almost yelled at him to stop. Then he began to pace toward her. At first she thought he was walking, but his steps were closer together and more deliberately placed. He was pacing off distance.

When he reached the upright column, he moved to the left approximately six feet from where he'd started and paced out to the edge again.

Ziko was frowning as he neared the dip in the floor. Before she could cry out an alarm, he skirted the area. He paced the distance all along the edge, his frown ever present.

As Ziko got further away from her, Gabrielle walked along the line of upright columns, touching each one under the pretense of resting against them. When she reached the pillar closest to the sloped floor, a vision filled her mind.

Once again, Roger Barrett stood studying the unfinished floor. A black-haired man stood beside him, and for a moment Gabrielle thought it was Christian Ziko. But when he turned to Barrett, she saw he was older than Christian, his face rounder, but the familial resemblance was distinctive. This must be Christian's brother, Paul, Barrett's best friend.

Christian's muttering shattered the vision like a stone dropping into a pool of water. "This can't be right."

She shook herself, eager to get back to the focus of her investigation. "What's not right?"

"I could swear it was thirty feet, but this is twenty-five."

"Maybe you measured incorrectly. Your feet aren't exactly accurate instruments."

"They're close enough, and I've never been wrong."

Gabrielle filed that little tidbit of information away. "Then maybe you remember the length incorrectly."

"No. I remember most of the specs on my drawings."

"Maybe you're remembering the first draft. How many times did you redraw the blueprints?"

His blue eyes narrowed. "Is that for your investigation?"

"I was trying to help."

"Three times."

"Then maybe you're remembering the first or second draft. I'm sure first plans have to allow for reality."

"Maybe." But he continued to frown.

"I've got a copy of the drawings in my car. Do you want to see them?" She couldn't believe she'd offered that to him. What was wrong with her?

"Yes, I'd like that."

"Are you through here?" Between the ragged edge of the floor and the knowledge the building might not be sound, her nerves were shredded. The sooner she got off this floor, the better.

"I guess." He looked around, as though trying to find something. He raked a hand through his hair with a jerky movement that looked like frustration.

Gabrielle headed for the exit, assuming Ziko would follow her. When she reached the door, he was right behind her. Once again he'd invaded her space. Her skin felt too tight, she was too warm and she was very conscious of the animal warmth of him. He smelled of soap and oddly enough, antiseptic. His nostrils flared slightly as though he was scenting her, too.

As he reached past her to take hold of the door, she noticed a raw red patch on the inside of his wrist.

"After you." He indicated the open door.

Gabrielle was mortified. She'd stood there gawking at him like a woman who'd never seen a man before. She'd never had a man's heat go to her head like strong liquor before. And for that man to be as inappropriate as Christian Ziko was humiliating. He wasn't even attracted to her.

Oh yes, he was.

No, he wasn't. Besides, he was probably guilty, so there was no future in this imaginary attraction.

She was very aware of Ziko behind her all the way down the stairs. She didn't want to speed up and risk taking a nasty tumble or let him know how nervous he was making her feel. Never let a suspect put you on the run. That gave them the upper hand.

At the first floor, Gabrielle turned toward the front door. But Ziko walked out into the atrium to the fallen girder, crunching through broken glass to reach it. He crouched beside the end of it, reaching out to touch something on its surface. She should probably move closer so she'd know what he was doing.

But he stood and once again paced off the length of the girder. At the end of it, he frowned and looked up toward the third floor. She didn't know what he was thinking, but whatever it was disturbed him. His scowl deepened. Then he turned and strode purposefully toward her. There was such an aura of violence around him she opened the outer door and got out of the way so he could stalk through it. But even the concrete courtyard wasn't enough room to hold his disquiet. He paced back and forth while she locked up the building until he stopped with a jerk.

"The blueprints?"

Gabrielle headed for the parking lot, where she unlocked the back of her Subaru Outback and handed a round cardboard tube to Ziko. While he pulled out the blueprints inside it, she noticed the heavy clouds were nearly black with impending rain. An ominous rumble nearby heralded the oncoming storm. She wondered why she hadn't heard thunder while she was inside the Densmore.

One fat drop decided her. "It's going to pour. We'd better get in my car if your want to look those over."

No sooner were they inside then the sprinkles turned into full-fledged rain. She turned on both map lights so he could better see the drawings.

"Here," Ziko pointed. "Hmph, twenty-five feet. I could have sworn it was longer."

"I told you the material matched the drawings." She tried to keep any accusation out of her voice. But it all came back to the drawing and who had drawn it. That's where the fault lay.

"I wouldn't do that. I wouldn't make a deathtrap."

"Maybe not intentionally." Oh, she was a sap. Ziko could be playing her for a fool. It was a good thing she worked with the structural end of investigations and not the people end, otherwise Michigan Casualty would lose millions each year as she was suckered by sob stories.

"So I'm guilty in your eyes." There was bitterness in his voice and pain in his blue eyes.

"I'm not your judge and jury."

"No, but your report will convict me." He rolled up the drawings and shoved them back in the cardboard tube before he handed it to her. "Thanks for letting me into the building."

He ran through the pouring rain to a Jeep parked close by. As he drove away, she started her car and the blast of air conditioning made a shiver run down her spine.

Or was it the lost look on his face that chilled her?

CHAPTER 3

Christian shivered with chill by the time he turned into the driveway of his condo in Bloomfield Hills. He'd held his emotions in check all the way home because he feared letting them lose anyplace public. He couldn't risk anyone seeing him have a possible breakdown and recognize who he was. Gabrielle Healey had enough nails for his coffin. He wouldn't give other people the chance to have more.

He cursed his stupidity. She'd told him who she was and what she was doing at the Densmore. She'd as much as told him she believed it was his fault. Yet he'd foolishly tried to change her mind. He'd been so sure about the measurement. He'd proven to her he was fallible, that he made mistakes. Now she was sure he'd made a fatal mistake on the Densmore.

After showering away the rain and the final taint of antiseptic from Crittenden, he dressed in black slacks, loafers and a navy button-down shirt with the sleeves rolled up. The stuffy, medicated feeling in his head was almost gone, making it much easier to think. He'd check out the blueprints of the Densmore at the office and let his partner know he was back on his feet again.

He'd finished eating a fast food sub sandwich when the doorbell rang. In case it was the press, having learned he was back in town, Christian checked the peephole first. Finding his brother Paul on his doorstep, he sighed. He'd hoped for a few hours reprieve. He let his brother in.

Paul's hair was as black as Christian's, only wavier, and his eyes were the same shade of Caribbean blue. He had a handsome face and an upper torso muscled from years of working construction. "What the hell are you doing here? You need to go back to Crittenden."

Christian closed the door behind his brother. "It's good to see you too, bro. I feel much better, thanks for asking. I'm sure Dr. Bergman must have told you that."

"Sean told me you asked—no, you demanded—to be released."

"I don't need to be there anymore. I passed all his tests for cognitive reasoning. Look, I'm washed, shaved, and dressed in clean clothes. I've been to the Densmore—"

"Jesus Christ, are you trying to have another breakdown? The Densmore is what started it the first time. Come with me. I'm taking you back to Crittenden before you crash." Paul tried to take hold of his arm.

Christian sidestepped his brother. "No, Paul. Nothing's going to happen to me this time."

"Kit, listen to me. You didn't see yourself before you went to Crittenden. It was so much like after our parents died, it hurt to look at you. You're not like other people. Your highs are higher and your lows are much lower. It's what makes you a brilliant architect. But the lows, Kit, the lows can kill you."

That comment made Christian angry. "I've never tried to commit suicide."

"Not actively, no. But lying in bed and not eating or drinking will achieve the same result eventually."

"I just ate lunch, so you don't have to worry about me."

"Baby brother, you're all I have left. I've been watching over you since Mom and Dad died. I don't want anything to happen to you."

Christian's heart swelled with love for his brother. When their parents died, Christian had thought because he was seventeen he was adult enough to live alone in their parent's house.

He'd been so wrong. When the truancy police finally tracked Paul down, Christian's depression was so deep he hadn't gotten out of bed in three days. Paul fought the state for custody of him, but in order to win, Paul had to have Christian committed for psychiatric treatment. He'd been hospitalized for months while the doctors helped him deal with his parents' deaths and his uncontrolled bipolar disorder.

When Christian got out of the hospital, he'd lived with Paul until college, having learned his brother knew better than he did. He'd followed Paul into the construction trade, listening to his brother's advice about becoming an architect so he could join Paul's friend's firm.

He knew Paul loved him, but the advice his brother gave now wasn't something Christian could follow. Going back to Crittenden was the wrong thing to do. He hated like hell to deny his brother anything, but this was his life, not Paul's.

"Nothing's going to happen to me, Paul. And I'm not going back to Crittenden." He led the way into the living room.

Paul followed with another argument. "But what about meds? Yours aren't strong enough."

Christian settled into a chair. "Don't worry. Dr. Bergman prescribed new meds before he released me."

That seemed to take the wind out of Paul's sails. "Oh. That's good. You've been letting your family doctor treat you for too long. It's time you let a psychiatrist take over." Paul ran a hand through his hair. "Kit, the mayor's pushing for a ruling about the Densmore. There's a grand jury investigating."

Christian stilled. "A grand jury?" Jesus, things had escalated while he was away. "But I didn't do anything."

Paul sank onto the couch near him. "They're looking for a scapegoat to blame. I don't know if they'll find anything they can use as evidence, but I can't risk you. If you're at Crittenden, they can't touch you."

Paul wanted him to hide? "Why should I hide if I'm innocent?"

"Sometimes the innocent get ground up in the wheels of justice. I don't want you in jail. I'd rather you were safe at Crittenden."

"God, is that what you think my choices are?" Christian sprang out of his chair and paced.

"Yes. Kit, you could be killed in jail, raped, beaten. Terrible things happen to innocent people there."

Christian turned away from his brother and scrubbed a hand down his face. His brother's words terrified him. He'd never thought it would come to jail. He'd designed a building, for God's sake. There had been a senseless, terrible accident. He hadn't taken a gun and shot those people. Jail. No, it wouldn't come to that.

Fool, get your head out of the clouds. Paul had said they wanted a scapegoat. But if Christian could find evidence of what happened, he could point the lynch mob in another direction.

"How long do we have before the grand jury makes a ruling?"

"I don't know, but if we leave for Crittenden now, it won't matter if the ruling comes down today. You'll be safe."

"I don't intend to hide at Crittenden. I'll investigate the Densmore collapse and find out what happened."

Paul stood and grabbed Christian's arm. His blue eyes snapped with anger. "Would you listen to yourself? There have been investigators all over the Densmore. They've probably already found any evidence there is. There's no time for you to play Hardy Boy. Get in the car."

Paul had never been angry with him before. It unsettled Christian, but he held firm and shook off his brother's hand. "I need to prove I'm innocent, Paul. Even to you." He held his breath, hoping his brother would deny it.

"What I believe doesn't matter. Other people won't believe you. I still love you. I'm always going to love you, no matter what."

Christian shook his head. "I can't hide. I want you to know I'm innocent. I'm going to prove it to you."

"That's insane, Kit. How are you going to do that?"

"I'm going to do what I should have done from the beginning of the project—I'm going to be involved. I swear on our parents' graves I'll find out what happened."

*

Gabrielle tossed her clipboard onto her desk at Michigan Casualty. She slid the cardboard tube full of blueprints onto the floor in the corner. What a day, and it wasn't even half over.

"Find anything new, Gabrielle?" Her boss, Cal Beyers, was a thirty-five-year-old black man on the fast track in management. He'd cut claims payouts by fifteen percent since he started in her department eighteen months ago. She didn't expect he'd be in her department much longer.

"Christian Ziko was on-site," she said.

His chocolate brown eyes widened and he came fully into her cubicle. "The bastard. What'd he want?"

"I think he wanted to see the building."

"He's probably looked at it every day for the past two weeks."

Gabrielle shook her head. "No, he says he's been out of town." That mystery still bothered her. Where had he gone?

Cal frowned. "Out of town doing what? What could be more important than having one of his buildings collapse?"

She'd wondered the same thing. "Maybe Barrett and Ziko have another building going up somewhere else."

"Then why didn't Barrett oversee it? He's been in town this whole time."

Gabrielle shrugged. "Maybe they thought it best if Ziko stayed out of sight for awhile."

"Then it had the reverse effect. So, what else did he say?"

"We actually went up to the third floor."

"The third floor. What the hell were you thinking? It's not safe. You could have been killed."

She knew her boss was right about the danger. "Nothing happened."

"Still, I thought you were more intelligent than that. Listen, I'm not telling you anything you probably haven't figured out for yourself, but I'm not going to be in this position much longer. I've been watching you lately, evaluating your performance, and I think you might be ready to step into my job when I'm promoted. Your work with the Densmore team has been outstanding."

A promotion? Gabrielle's heartbeat quickened. In the twelve years she'd worked here, watching managers cycle through her office on their way up the ladder, they'd never once promoted from within the investigative department. She wanted a chance at Cal's job.

"But you can't take chances like you did today," Cal said. "Initiative is fine, but stupidity won't get you promoted."

"I'll think before I act next time."

He leaned in close enough that she could smell his musk aftershave. "And if there's anything Ziko told you that assures Michigan Casualty won't have to pay a dime, I think both of us will be changing offices. Was there anything?"

"He thought the girders were supposed to have been longer. But that was probably on the initial draft, not the final one."

Cal raised an eyebrow. "So there's no proof of what he claimed?"

"No. The girders are the same size specified in the blueprints."

"Did he say anything else?"

He'd proclaimed his innocence. But Cal didn't want to hear that—he wanted a fall guy. He was chomping at the bit to get out of her department.

"No."

"Too bad. So, will I have your team's report on the Densmore soon?"

"Yeah. I've got to assemble all the data, cross all my t's and dot all my i's, but you'll have it in a couple of days."

"Will I be happy?"

"I'm pretty sure you'll get a new desk."

His bright white teeth were quite a contrast to his dark skin. "That's great. I knew I could count on you." He turned and strode off.

Gabrielle wished she felt as content. All her data pointed to a flawed design, but her meeting with Ziko had left her disturbed. Had he been so single-mindedly focused he couldn't see his design wouldn't work? Maybe he was so arrogant he couldn't fathom that something he designed could fail. Or maybe he was as facile a liar as the rest of the men in her life had been. Some had dumped her to her face, but the majority had slunk away and either avoided her calls or told her pretty lies about why they couldn't make time for her.

Maybe she was the dreamer, thinking any man was accommodating enough to want a woman who'd know by touching him that he'd kissed another woman. Her father had left her mother for that very reason. Gabrielle had only been four at the time and hadn't known better than to ask her Daddy why he'd been kissing that blond woman while Mommy was at work. The divorce that followed had been bitter, with her Daddy calling her "that freak." She hadn't seen him since.

Years later, her grandmother, a Native American wise woman, had admitted it was one of the reasons why she didn't live with Gabrielle's grandfather. He hadn't wanted her to practice her "witchcraft" in his house. So she'd chosen to live without him in her life, surviving in a cabin in Michigan's Upper Peninsula not far from the Indian reservation where she'd grown up.

She'd warned Gabrielle what a curse others thought it was to have the sight, how hard it made life for a woman. It had certainly made life miserable for the women in her family. And Gabrielle had found out the hard way for herself with a string of broken relationships. No, men couldn't accept a woman who was different.

At thirty-two, she hadn't completely resigned herself to spinsterhood, but in a few more years and a few more failed relationships, she'd have to. She'd be very lucky to have a management position to fill up the empty hours of her life where a husband and children would never be. So she'd better make sure there were no other suspects besides Christian Ziko in the Densmore case.

*

Christian exited the elevator on the top floor of the Piedmont building in Troy where Barrett and Ziko Architectural had its offices. The company was home and Roger was like family, because he was Paul's best friend, his frat brother from the University of Michigan. Christian pushed through the glass double doors with the gold stenciling on it. Immediately he was enveloped by the familiar scents of blueprint ink, wood, and French vanilla roast coffee.

The firm's receptionist/secretary, Brittany Franks, looked up from her typing with a smile on her face that widened to surprise when she saw him. "Christian, you're back."

She sprang out of her chair and leaned over the curved reception desk until he feared for the security of the buttons on her tight blouse. Brittany was a very well-endowed young woman.

"Did you enjoy your trip?" There were layers of questions under her question.

He wondered for a moment what trip she was talking about. Then he realized that must have been how Roger explained his absence. "It was relaxing." Before she could ask further questions, he asked one of his own. "Is Roger here?"

"Yes, in his office."

"I'll need to see the Densmore file, if you could put it on my desk."

A little frown beetled her perfectly arched brows. "Sure."

When Christian entered Roger's office, his partner looked up and sighed, tossing his mechanical pencil onto his desk. His thin blondish hair was artfully streaked with lighter shades of blond. The blue of his eyes was almost colorless, it was so light. His shirt was open at the throat, displaying the gold necklace his twenty-four-year-old second wife had given him. The effect was to make him appear a decade younger than forty-four.

"Close the door," Roger said.

Christian did as he was bid.

"Paul told me you were out of Crittenden. He also said he was taking you back. So what the hell are you doing here?"

Christian bit down on his irritation. This wasn't the welcome he'd expected. "I feel fine and I'm ready to come back to work. It can't have been easy for you holding down the fort while I was away."

"No, it wasn't. I know you'd like to think you're ready, Kit, but you're a liability to me right now. I don't have time to worry about whether you'll be here to finish any new projects we start or whether you'll have a breakdown on a jobsite."

"I won't."

"You can't prove that. You left against medical advice. Do your brother and me a favor and go back to Crittenden until you're well."

Christian fisted his hands at his sides. "I am well. And it wasn't against medical advice. Dr. Bergman agreed I was fit to leave."

Roger rubbed his temples. "Are you on your meds?"

Christian gritted his teeth. "Yes."

"Sean said your meds are years out of date."

It was hard for Christian to orient himself to the fact his psychiatrist, Dr. Sean Bergman, was Roger's good friend. But that didn't give Sean the right to break HIPAA rules about Christian's treatment. Only Paul was privy to that information. Christian would have to handle that problem later.

"You don't have to worry about that anymore because he prescribed new ones."

"Sean and I discussed bipolar and how it's treated with today's medicine. He says it's trial and error to get the right mix of meds to control the symptoms. You feel fine today, but what if the new medicine's not right for you? And what if you skip a day? He says it's important for people who suffer from severe depression to take their medication daily to prevent suicidal spirals."

Christian had thought the people he trusted most trusted him. It was infuriating to know what they actually thought and that his breakdown was partly to blame for their doubts.

"My depression's not that bad, Roger, and I plan to take my medicine every day from now on."

"I'm not saying these things to hurt you, Kit, but to show you how important it is to let Sean and the other doctors figure out a medical regimen that works for you. Go back to Crittenden. In a few weeks when you're stabilized, Sean will release you."

"I can get the same care as an outpatient. I need to be free to figure out why the Densmore collapsed."

Roger paled. "What?"

"No one's trying to prove I'm innocent, so I'll have to do it myself."

Roger stiffened. "Absolutely not. You wouldn't last an hour digging through the Densmore records."

"I'm not going to have a breakdown looking over that file."

"You're not—"

"Roger?" Brittany's voice blared over the intercom.

Roger stabbed the intercom button on his phone. "Not now."

"Roger, the police are here." Her voice quavered slightly.

Roger ran a hand through his thinning hair. "Jesus. What now?" He punched the intercom again. "Send them back."

He looked up at Christian. "Do me a favor and go back to Crittenden."

A knock on the door cut off Christian's scathing comment. Brittany escorted in two uniformed policemen and two men with police badges on their suits. The uniforms eyed Christian with cold, curious eyes.

"What can I do for you, officers?" Roger asked.

"Are you Christian Ziko?" one of the uniforms asked Christian.

"Yes."

"By order of the grand jury, you're under arrest."

CHAPTER 4

"Under arrest? For what?" *Don't panic.* There had to be some mistake. Christian and Paul had talked about jail, but not in the context of police officers arresting him today.

One uniformed cop advanced toward him. "For suspicion of fraud and malfeasance pertaining to the construction of the Densmore Building."

One of the police detectives waved a white paper. "We've got a warrant for your arrest."

The uniformed cop tried to take hold of Christian's arm, but Christian shook the man off.

"I'm innocent. I didn't do anything fraudulent in designing the Densmore."

"That's for a jury to decide. The grand jury thought there was sufficient evidence to indict you. I'm afraid we're going to have to handcuff you and take you down to the station."

"That's not necessary." Christian took another step away from the cop. "If you want me to go with you, I'll go peaceably without handcuffs."

The cop reached for him again. "Just give me your wrists."

His partner was almost within reach. Christian felt cornered. He didn't want to be handcuffed. He didn't want to go to jail.

"Kit, let the policemen do their jobs," Roger said. His face was grim, his mouth pinched in a tight line.

"No. I didn't do anything wrong." Christian's breathing was coming too fast.

The first uniform grabbed his arm. Before Christian could react, the cop slammed Christian face first against the office wall. As Christian tried to rear back, the policeman jammed his billy club against his neck.

Panic was a wild animal inside him. "I'm innocent!" The wall muffled his shout.

"Save it for the trial," the cop growled.

The other policeman moved behind him and cuffed him rather roughly.

"Roger, do something," Christian demanded as the cops turned him around to face the room once more.

One of the detectives handed Roger a piece of paper. "Roger Barrett, this is a search warrant to seize all documents pertaining to the Densmore." He slapped a second piece of paper into Roger's hand. "And this is a subpoena to appear in court to testify."

Roger's face turned beet red as he stared at the subpoena. Christian hoped his partner would finally get angry enough to intervene. Christian was becoming claustrophobic. Memories of his last days at Crittenden and being restrained threatened to panic him. The handcuffs rubbed across his still-tender wrists.

"Fine," Roger said through gritted teeth, tossing the subpoena on his desk. "We'll cooperate. Kit, go with them."

Christian couldn't believe what he was hearing. He strained against the two policemen who held him between them. "But it's not right. I didn't kill those people. I didn't do anything wrong."

"I'll call Paul." Roger's face had returned to its original color. "You won't be at the police station long. Just sit tight and Paul will come bail you out."

The two uniformed cops hauled Christian toward the door as the detectives spoke to Roger.

"We're going to need access to Mr. Ziko's computer and all his records."

The uniforms tugged Christian's resisting body out the door and down the hall. He dragged his feet, trying to delay them, trying to stop them, anything not to have to go to jail.

"Mr. Ziko!" Brittany gasped, her eyes wide.

"It's all a mistake," Christian said as he was marched past her.

The cops ogled her as they tugged on his arms, but any hope her distracting presence would make them loosen their hold on him was for naught.

Once the glass doors of Barrett and Ziko had closed behind them, the cop on the right jerked on Christian's arm. "You want us to add resisting arrest to the charges?"

"It's my life we're talking about, my freedom. You bet I'm going to resist."

"We're going to be out of sight soon and nobody at the precinct is going to care what shape you arrive in. After all, you killed all those people."

Christian stilled, a cold knot of dread tightening in his belly. These men didn't care what happened to him. They already thought he was guilty because a grand jury had indicted him.

"I didn't kill anybody," he said in a quiet voice. He wanted to tone down the officers' hostility. With his arms cuffed behind him, he couldn't fight off a billy club if they decided to take their anger out on him.

"Listen, Ziko," the second cop said. "Just come peaceably. We've got a job to do. It's not up to us to decide your guilt or innocence. All we have to do is take you to the station and book you. You'll be released when you post bail and then you and your lawyer can decide how to defend you."

The elevator dinged and the door opened. Christian let them lead him into the car and held his breath when the door shut, hoping they didn't still think beating him into submission was a good idea.

His cooperative behavior must have appeased them, because the trip through the lobby and out to the waiting patrol car was uneventful. But he hoped Paul hurried.

*

"A hundred thousand dollars for bail? That's insane." Christian gripped the bars of his jail cell hard as he faced Paul through them.

"That's what I said." Paul ran a hand through his black hair, tousling the already mussed strands.

"Can you get that much money?"

"Kit, normally I could. But this damn rain has delayed all my current projects. You know construction work always has liquid cash problems."

"Can you get a loan against your house?"

Paul sighed. "I didn't want to have to tell you this, but Pam filed for divorce. She's tied up all our personal assets and is trying to get her hands on the business assets. I don't have any personal money right now."

"Jesus, Paul. You and Pam seemed so happy." Other people got divorced, not Paul.

"Seemed is the right word. I was working too many hours. She had all her social activities. We didn't see much of each other."

"Can't you get counseling or try working on your marriage?"

Paul shook his head. "Pam doesn't want to. I have to talk to her through her attorney."

Christian frowned. "That doesn't sound like Pam."

"It doesn't matter. Because of her, all my assets are tied up."

"What about my house? Can you get the money using it?"

"I don't know if you've got enough equity in it. You just bought it last year."

Christian gripped the bars harder. "Will you try?"

"All right, but it's going to take time."

"It's already been two hours."

"I'm sorry. I needed to check my financial situation."

Christian wanted to shake his brother until he moved faster. "I can't stand being in here. It's like," he dropped his voice to a whisper, "Crittenden."

Paul leaned close to the bars. "I warned you, Kit. I told you to go back there. You're too vulnerable on the outside."

Christian rattled the bars. "I don't want to be locked up anywhere. I have to be free to prove my innocence."

"I'll do what I can as fast as I can, but it's been a really bad spring."

"Don't I know it."

"Try to relax. The last thing we need is for you to get upset. I'll be back as soon as I can." Paul gripped Christian's arm, his features strained, before he turned and left.

Christian returned to his uncomfortable bunk. With Paul gone and Roger tied up at the office, Christian felt alone and friendless. The cops thought he was where he belonged and the press was happy he was behind bars—there had been a veritable feeding frenzy when he'd been brought in.

He was lucky Paul could even break away from his building sites to post his bail. Christian's life had been like that, too, for the past year. His company had won numerous contracts where they were architect as well as contractor. There were too many details to oversee and not enough hours in the day.

He and Roger had discussed taking on another partner, but there had never been time to interview prospects. So they had tried to handle the load, and the Densmore tragedy resulted.

Flinging himself to his feet, he paced the small confines of the cell. He felt trapped, like some wild animal. He was afraid he'd never be free again. He'd go crazy if he was sentenced to a cell like this for years.

He needed help to clear himself. A picture of Gabrielle Healey came to mind. With her logical mind and intense probing, she'd be able to find the evidence he needed. But she was the enemy. Even now, her report might have helped condemn him.

But she'd seemed so adamant about learning the truth.

The truth as she saw it.

Christian turned to stalk in the other direction. She would never help him. Only if he had some radical new piece of information would she listen to him.

If only those girders hadn't matched her drawings. He'd thought for sure somehow there'd been a mix-up in materials. But they had matched.

He paused. No. The drawing had matched the materials.

Christian kept a back-up copy of all his blueprints in his home computer so he could work from home. If he had a copy of a later drawing that didn't match the materials, Gabrielle would want to see it. She'd want to help him.

Damn. He had to get out of here so he could check the blueprints in his computer. He was sure it was the place to start.

Where the hell was Paul with his bail?

*

At a little after eight the next morning, Paul bailed Christian out of jail and dropped him at his house with a fast food breakfast and a plea to call if Christian changed his mind about being admitted to Crittenden.

With coffee in hand, Christian opened his computer file of blueprints, found the ones for the Densmore and checked the dates. Paging through the different schematics, he found the one for the third floor and traced the support beams until his finger underlined the length of the girders.

Thirty feet.

All the air left his lungs. His coffee cup hit the desk and nearly spilled the hot liquid. Jesus Christ. He'd been right. Excitement filled his veins, making him jump up and shout. He was innocent, and here was the proof. God, he was innocent.

Then reality struck him, hard. The building had been built with twenty-five-foot girders, not thirty. But here was the drawing, the proof. Gabrielle Healey had said the materials met the drawings specs, but how could they have?

Wait, he'd looked at the drawing in her car. He'd seen with his own eyes the measurement of twenty-five feet. Who'd drawn that drawing? He didn't remember doing it.

As quickly as he could, he checked the other files. Never had he drawn the third floor guiders at under thirty feet. They needed the length to spread the tension out and across. That's how the third floor could appear to defy gravity.

Jesus. That's why the third floor hadn't defied gravity.

CHAPTER 5

Gabrielle's desk phone rang, interrupting her perfectly worded thoughts on Christian Ziko's guilt for her final report.

"Damn." She wrung her hands, trying to get the words back. When that didn't work, she answered the phone. "Cost Containment, Healey."

"Ms. Healey, it's Christian Ziko. I've found something you need to see."

Speak of the devil. "What did you find?"

"The original blueprints."

"So? You told me you'd made several revised drawings."

"This is the drawing DesignCorp tested. The one that didn't fail. Guess what length the girders are?"

Was he playing games with her? "Why don't you just tell me what length they are?"

"Thirty feet."

"Then it must be an older drawing. We both know the girders are twenty-five feet."

"I'm telling you, this is the drawing I was using the day we broke ground on the Densmore, after DesignCorp approved the design for construction."

"You know as well as I do plans change during construction to accommodate unforeseen problems. Every changed drawing is filed with the appropriate people."

"But this was the only drawing tested by DesignCorp."

"I'm sure I saw a certificate from DesignCorp on the final blueprints." She dug frantically through her files.

"No, that's not possible. I couldn't make this design work at a shorter length."

44

"But you drew the changes."

"No, I didn't."

"It's your signature on the blueprints I showed you, just like on every other blueprint associated with the Densmore."

"That's not possible."

"It is." Too bad she didn't have a free hand to unroll the blueprints. But her memory was excellent.

"Ms. Healey, I know that design. I put my heart and soul into it."

"I look at facts, Mr. Ziko, and the evidence shows your signature on the revised drawing."

"I want to see that drawing."

She sighed. He was going to become obsessive about it. "Listen, Mr. Ziko, your firm has a copy of the drawing. Look it up."

"The cops confiscated it."

She thought quickly. "There's a copy on file with the county. I'm sure you can go to the city planner's office and look it up."

"Why don't you bring your copy with you when you come over?"

"I'm not coming to see you." God, wouldn't that be a conflict of interest? She could picture Cal having an apoplectic fit.

"I need to show you the date on this drawing. I need to prove my innocence." His voice was insistent.

"I'm hardly a neutral party, Mr. Ziko."

"So you're not interested in my innocence?"

"That drawing doesn't prove you're innocent, while my drawing actually makes you look guilty. So do the DesignCorp test results."

"There's no talking to you. Your mind's made up. You've reached a verdict and you're not going to accept any evidence that doesn't support your theory, despite what you told me. I'm sorry I called." He hung up.

Ziko's accusation stung. She'd always been fair and impartial in her investigations and had never turned in a biased report to

Michigan Casualty. But he was a guilty man desperate to use any method to get someone to listen to his pitiful plea. He thought she'd be easier to sway than the grand jury.

Well, he was wrong. She pulled out the documents to confirm her assertions. Unrolling the blueprints, she carefully traced his signature on the bottom of each page. He'd drawn these, and then he'd lied to her about it. Why?

Gabrielle sorted through the numerous papers until she found the DesignCorp report. It didn't give specs, just named the Densmore project.

It was a fill-in-the-blanks type form with DesignCorp's logo and address at the top. It listed the tolerances to which the design was tested and the parameters within which it passed. All routine. They needed a better printer, because even though she was looking at a copy of a copy, it appeared hand typed, not computer generated. Probably another case of cost cutting, where the company should upgrade but didn't. She saw it a lot in her investigations—old wiring, buildings not up to code, insufficient smoke alarms—and all because building owners didn't want to part with their profits.

No, Ziko was wrong. Hers was the drawing used to build the Densmore, and it was his design that failed.

She pulled her keyboard toward her. In twenty-five minutes she had completed her summary and condemned Christian Ziko's design as the reason for the Densmore's collapse. Cal would be extremely pleased. If he kept his word, she'd be sitting in his office soon and receiving a fat raise. Yet she hesitated, saving the file instead of sending it to Cal. She hoped he hadn't been stringing her along about that promotion.

*

Christian slammed down the phone. "Damn." He'd thought Gabrielle Healey would jump at the news about the blueprint. But she'd shrugged it off. Didn't anybody want the truth? Didn't anybody care if an innocent man went to jail? It seemed like no one did.

He had enough time to visit the City Planning office before his appointment with Paul's frat brother, Bryce Gannon, the hotshot defense attorney.

As he drove out of the garage, Christian's Jeep was immediately surrounded by people with cameras and microphones.

"Mr. Ziko, do you have any words for the families?"

"Mr. Ziko, is it true your business is in financial trouble over the Densmore fiasco?"

They were jackals, the worst kind of predators, circling the injured, waiting to get in a kill shot. He shuddered and drove past them without stopping.

That last reporter's question made his chest tighten. Was his company in financial jeopardy because of the Densmore? He hadn't discussed anything with Roger in the past few weeks. Yesterday they hadn't gotten past their argument. He needed to know if Barrett and Ziko was in trouble.

While he navigated the streets, he called his office, but Brittany told him Roger was out.

Christian had a brainstorm, "Are the police gone?"

"Yeah. They took all our files on the Densmore and they made a real mess doing it."

"Did they take the blueprints?"

"Yep, everything."

"Damn. I'm on my way to City Planning to look at what they've got on file, but I was hoping not to have to go there."

"What do you think you'll find?"

"I don't know. But I want to see if I signed the blueprints."

"You must have. You designed the building."

"I'm going to see for myself. Thanks, Brittany."

At the City Planning office, Christian knew the man at the counter. Josh Morgan was thirty-something, with nut-brown hair and a look of dismay on his face. His brown eyes went wide and his mouth dropped open.

"Christian Ziko." He said it like he couldn't believe it.

"Josh. I need to see the building plans for the Densmore Building."

If Josh had been dismayed before, now he was outraged. His face reddened. "What the hell for?"

"I'm trying to prove I'm innocent."

"I don't think I can let you back here."

"Dammit, Josh, everybody making a case against me has a copy of the damn drawing. How can I defend myself if I don't know what I'm defending against?"

"There is no defense against what you did."

"But I didn't kill anybody and I'm going to prove it. Are you going to let me back there or will it make you feel better if an innocent man goes to jail?"

Josh glowered, but then he reached below the counter and the door buzzed.

"Thanks." Christian took a seat in one of the conference rooms set up for people to look at blueprints.

When Josh delivered the drawings, Christian paged through them until he located the one of the third floor. His finger traced over to the lower right-hand corner. There was his signature.

A wave of despair washed over him, and he dropped his head into his hands. It couldn't be possible. He couldn't be a murderer. No. A black pit opened up in front of him, threatening to engulf him. For a moment his vision darkened. He remembered every project he'd ever worked on, remembered lovingly sculpting the Densmore. But this revision…his mind was a blank.

Christian swam out of the dark. He wouldn't have changed this drawing, not this one. He knew how he drew lines and angles, joints and fittings, how he wrote numbers. Frowning, he traced over the dimensions again. This wasn't his work.

Elation practically doubled him over. He crossed his arms across his midsection, barely preventing an animal groan from escaping his lips. He wasn't a murderer.

No, he was an accessory to murder. He'd handed the gun to whoever pulled the trigger. He'd signed off on the work. Jesus.

He straightened up and stared at the unknown lines again and then he looked down at his signature, but he couldn't recall a single instance of signing off on a drawing without looking at it first.

As he looked even closer, he noticed the signature seemed shaky. He'd always had fine motor control, so it might just be a poor quality copy. Quickly he grabbed a magnifying glass. Under the larger magnification, he could see the letters weren't fluid, as though the person writing it had stopped midway through and started again.

His heart lurched and then began beating more rapidly. It wasn't his signature. He drew in his breath. Someone had forged his signature.

His first thought was Roger, but this wasn't Roger's work. He had a heavier hand when he designed, very confident and bold, and he wrote his numbers differently.

So who'd drawn it and signed it?

If Roger had authorized it, and he must have, why hadn't he said anything to Christian about it and why hadn't he done the work himself? He should never have given this to anyone else to work on, and if he had, why hadn't he signed his own name to it once the revision was finished? It didn't make sense.

So who else at the firm could have revised the drawing and why forge Christian's name to it? He didn't think Paul's son Jeremy would do it. As far as he knew, Brittany couldn't do architectural drawings. That only left the college intern who'd been with them for a semester, but the Densmore was far above internship level work.

Before Christian could go crazy trying to find an answer, he needed proof this wasn't his signature. The cops had handwriting experts. He should take the drawing to them and ask for their help. But after yesterday's handling, he wasn't sure how much cooperation they would give him.

Maybe Gabrielle Healey could help him. But first he needed to update Roger on what he'd found. Christian called the office hoping Roger was back from his meeting. But the answering machine came on immediately. Where was everybody? A glance at his watch showed it wasn't even lunchtime yet.

Josh poked his head into the room.

"I'll need a copy of this page," Christian told him.

As Josh stalked off with the blueprint, Christian dialed Gabrielle's number. When she answered, he identified himself and told her, "It's not my signature on the drawing."

She made a sound of exasperation. "Of course it is."

"No, it's not. I checked it under a magnifying glass. Someone forged my name, probably by tracing a copy they already had. I need a handwriting expert to verify what I'm saying. Can you help me, because I don't think the police will."

Gabrielle blew out her breath. "All right." He heard papers shuffling on her end. "Call Alex Kernfelter at this number and tell him I recommended you to him." She rattled off the number.

"You don't want to call him first?"

"No. I can't get directly involved with this."

"I see." He was still persona non grata with her. "Well, thanks for the name anyway."

"Mr. Ziko?"

"What?"

"Please let me know the results."

"I'll have Mr. Kernfelter call you."

When he hung up from her, he felt distinctly bereft. How strange, when every time he spoke to her she didn't believe him.

Christian called Kernfelter and agreed to meet him in twenty minutes if he didn't have to duck reporters.

He felt Josh's stare burning into his back as he left with a copy of the drawing. He'd thought it would be easy to prove his innocence, but people didn't seem to want to hear what he had to say. He was guilty until proven innocent, apparently.

As he exited the County offices, he was mobbed by a handful of reporters.

"What are you doing here, Mr. Ziko?"

"Were you trying to get in to see the mayor, Mr. Ziko?"

"What's that in your hand?" An eagle-eyed reporter spotted the drawing.

Christian gripped his evidence tighter. He wondered if telling the reporters what he'd found would be to his benefit. But he needed to warn Roger first. He didn't want his partner blindsided by this.

So he pushed his way through the reporters to his Jeep without saying a word. They were persistent buzzards, though, firing questions at him despite his lack of response.

He drove out of the parking lot, heading away from the crowded downtown area. He thought one of the reporters followed him, because a black SUV kept pace with him one car back.

Christian turned right at the next stop light. The black SUV turned right a moment later. Damn reporters. He gunned the Jeep and turned left in front of oncoming traffic. Horns blared. He made another right at the next corner and then a second right a few moments later. There was no sign of the black SUV. Good.

Kernfelter's company, Forensic Sciences, Inc., occupied the entire first floor of a two-story brick building. A matronly woman manned the front desk.

"My name's Christian Ziko. Mr. Kernfelter is expecting me."

"Yes. Let me buzz him. Oh, there you are, sir." Her gaze swung to the right where a middle-aged man with sharp, dark eyes and crisp brown hair leaned past her so Christian could see him.

"Mr. Ziko, come around to the door. I'll meet you there."

As promised, Kernfelter opened the inner door as Christian reached it. The older man ushered him through. As soon as the door was closed behind him, Kernfelter stuck out his hand and introduced himself.

Alex Kernfelter had a strong grip. He was eye level with Christian and his gaze was piercing. "Come into my office before we discuss anything. Our staff is extremely discreet, but I want privacy when we begin."

Kernfelter waved him to a seat in a brown leather and wood chair. "Do you think someone sabotaged the Densmore, perhaps as a way to destroy you or your firm?"

"No, I don't think so."

Kernfelter's mouth twisted. "I didn't want to believe it, but I wondered. Let me see the drawing."

Christian unrolled the drawing across the desk. Pointing to the signature, he stated, "There. If I had to guess, I'd say somebody traced my handwriting."

Alex studied the writing with a magnifying glass, before lifting his head. "It's certainly not a steady hand. Someone like you who's young and healthy wouldn't ordinarily write with a shaky hand. I'll need several samples of your signature and to see your driver's license and credit card signatures for comparison as well."

Christian pulled out his wallet and deposited the requested items on top the drawing. By then, Kernfelter had a blank piece of paper he handed Christian.

"Write your name ten times. Write as you normally would when you sign a blueprint, at whatever speed you would usually use. Don't think about what you're doing, just write."

Christian did as he was told. It was difficult not to concentrate on making his name legible, or to want his signature to appear different than the one on the drawing. When he was finished, Kernfelter took the page and compared it to the signatures on his driver's license and credit cards.

Christian held his breath as the handwriting expert checked back and forth between what Christian had provided and what was written on the drawing. The man studied all the signatures for a number of minutes. Finally, he sat back in his chair and laid the magnifying glass down.

"You're right. It looks like somebody traced your signature, but you didn't write it."

Christian's breath whooshed out. He took another deep one to steady himself. His hand was shaking as he ran it over his face. "I knew I wouldn't have signed off on this drawing. Not this project. It was too important to me."

"You're going to need me to testify about this in court. I wanted someone to pay for the deaths of those young people at the Densmore, but I want it to be the guilty person. Do you know who did it?"

Christian shook his head. "No. Chances are it was someone at my firm, like an intern, but I won't know until I ask."

Kernfelter's dark brows lifted. "You're going to do your own investigation?"

Christian shrugged. "I have to. Nobody else seems to want to."

"Your lawyer will want to get a deposition from me. Who's representing you?"

"Bryce Gannon. I'm supposed to meet him this afternoon."

"Give him my number. I'll expect to hear from him."

"Can you do me a favor, Mr. Kernfelter?"

"Sure, but call me Alex."

"Would you call Gabrielle Healey and tell her what you found. She asked that you call her."

"Certainly. Why don't I do it now while you're here?" He picked up the phone and dialed.

"Cost Containment, Healey." Gabrielle's voice spilled into the room through the speaker.

"Gabrielle, it's Alex Kernfelter. I've got Christian Ziko with me on speaker phone."

Christian heard her audible intake of breath.

"What do you think?" she asked, her voice full of caution.

"Someone forged his name on the drawing. I'll testify to it in court."

"God. I didn't believe him. Mr. Ziko, I'm so sorry."

Christian felt slightly mollified. "I told you I didn't do it."

"I know."

"I'm going to find out who did. I don't believe the police will help me. Will you?"

Her sigh gusted over the phone. "Yes."

CHAPTER 6

What was she doing? Gabrielle asked herself as she hung up the phone from talking to Christian Ziko. Was she crazy to agree to help him try to prove his innocence?

Yes, most definitely. Cal Beyers's words about not paying on the Densmore claim echoed in her mind. And that promotion was riding on her report, a report that now had to be rewritten. Although if forgery was involved, Michigan Casualty still wouldn't have to pay on the claim. But she needed to know the name of the guilty party or parties almost as badly as Christian Ziko did.

Was she letting her wayward thoughts and feelings for the man sway her decisions? She'd never done that before, but she'd never felt such a pull toward another person. He'd burrowed past her defenses with his vulnerable need and she couldn't allow him to drill any deeper. That he was male was all the more reason to steer clear of him.

"Will you be much longer on your report?" Cal Beyers asked.

She jerked, startled out of her disturbing thoughts. She hoped her guilt wasn't written on her face. "I'm not sure." Wait, hadn't he already asked her that question a few hours ago?

"I've got another claim I need investigated that's right up your alley. I thought I'd check and see how long until you're free before I assign it to someone else."

She looked away so he couldn't see the doubt in her eyes. He'd never checked on her availability before. What was the hurry to settle this case? Was there an opening in the company Cal wanted that she hadn't heard about yet? If so, the Densmore case might be the deciding factor in his getting the promotion…if Michigan Casualty didn't have to pay on the claim.

"I have to check one more thing before I can close the case."

"Something new since this morning?" His gaze pierced her, searching for the truth. His sharp tone hinted there'd better not be anything new.

She didn't want to have to explain the forged signature to him, because then she'd have to discuss it with him in-depth, and right now she didn't have enough facts to do that.

"Just something I have to check out. Nothing to worry about."

"That's good. Well, I'll assign this new claim to someone else then." He waited a moment longer, then he turned and walked away.

Gabrielle let out the breath she'd been holding and her shoulders slumped a little. She'd never been afraid at work before. Of course, she'd never had to hide anything major like this when everything she wanted was riding on the outcome.

She was a hands-on investigator, not just because she was clairvoyant, but because she was thorough, so she did the legwork and checked the paperwork herself. She couldn't allow Christian Ziko to do his own investigation and report the results to her. It didn't sound like he'd be willing to do that with her either.

That left working together. His pain-filled blue eyes floated into her memory. His slumped shoulders as he looked at his shattered dreams pulled at her. Dammit, working with him would be a major mistake.

When the phone rang five minutes later, she knew as she touched the receiver it was Ziko on the phone.

"It's Christian Ziko. I need a favor."

Already it began. She sighed. "What?"

"The cops confiscated all our files. I need to know who the subcontractors were on the Densmore."

"Your lawyer will get copies of everything."

"I can't wait weeks while this cloud of suspicion hangs over my head. I need to begin looking at people who could have changed the drawing right away."

"Why don't you begin at Barrett and Ziko? The person more than likely works there."

"No one's there right now. In the meantime, I thought I'd get the list from you."

"Mr. Ziko, you do realize my even speaking to you puts me in an awkward position. You're still the main suspect as far as the grand jury's concerned." And as far as her employer was concerned, that made him off limits to her except to interview for her report.

"But you know better."

"True, but no one else does."

"Ms. Healey, no one else seems to give a damn about me. My partner, who does give a damn, had to give up his records. Please, at least read me the list of company names."

She sighed again. Dammit, he was right. She was the only one who knew he had nothing to do with the Densmore collapse, and she could help him prove it. Well, here was her chance.

"Have you had lunch, Mr. Ziko?"

"Lunch?" He sounded puzzled. "No."

"Fine. I'll meet you somewhere for lunch and give you the information. Where are you?"

Ziko was still at Kernfelter's office, not far away. So Gabrielle gave him directions and he agreed to meet her in less than twenty minutes. When she hung up, she dropped her head in her hand.

What was she doing? She had the perfect opportunity to snag a job promotion she desperately needed, and she was trying to throw it away.

But what else could she do? Her job was to unearth the facts and make decisions based on those facts. Someone forged a document on which the Densmore was built. It was a fact, a lead. She had to follow it.

Gabrielle was pretty sure she'd chosen a restaurant far enough away from Michigan Casualty that she wouldn't meet any of her co-workers there. As she pulled into the restaurant parking lot, she looked for Ziko's black Cherokee. Not spying it, she gave a sigh of relief. She needed a few moments to compose herself before seeing him.

When Ziko walked in, the slump of despair was gone, replaced by an intensity almost palpable. This was a man on a mission. His blue gaze zeroed in on her like a heat-seeking missile. He strode in her direction, reaching her in only a few steps.

As he slid into the booth, his knee bumped hers. A vision, unwanted and unwelcome, appeared in her mind.

Christian Ziko stood at the edge of Lake Michigan staring up at the Mackinaw Bridge that connected the Lower Peninsula to the Upper Peninsula. He was a young man, possibly still in his late teens. His black hair touched his shoulders in back. The way he stared at the bridge, with a combination of awe and intense eagerness, reminded Gabrielle of his expression when he entered the restaurant. Here was the man who wanted to build great things. And she knew already, even at that young age, Ziko was in architectural school.

Ziko moved his knee and the vision dissolved. Gabrielle made a show of reaching for her menu while her emotions heaved. She'd wanted a career in architecture, but a love affair with a college classmate went sour when she revealed her clairvoyance to him. Unable to cope with seeing him and his condemning eyes each day, she'd changed her major to construction engineering. So Ziko had gone on to fulfill his dreams, and she…she hadn't.

"Thanks for meeting me. I didn't expect your offer."

Gabrielle laid her menu back on the table. "Once Alex Kernfelter ruled your signature a forgery, I decided I needed to become personally involved in the investigation. If I'd found it out myself, I wouldn't hesitate to continue looking for the truth."

"I have no intention of stepping aside for you to run your investigation, if that's why you asked me to meet you."

"I hadn't planned to ask you to."

"Good." He smiled for the first time, and it changed his whole face, transforming it into a thing of beauty. His features softened as much as she thought they probably ever did. Gabrielle's breath caught. Even more than his vulnerability, his happiness riveted her attention. She'd seen the look on his face when he was designing and been captivated. But this sudden glow was enough to discombobulate any living, breathing woman.

Even as she watched, his smile faded and she wanted to voice her protest at the unfairness. She wondered what it would be like to see him smile every day.

Whoa, where had that thought come from? But she continued to stare as he studied his menu. His face was triangular, his eyes deep set, his nose slender and straight and his jaw stubborn. It was a face of determination and intensity, of character and passion. A compelling face.

The waiter arrived and Gabrielle was glad to be distracted from her survey of Ziko. After taking their orders, he departed as quietly as he'd arrived.

"So you're going to investigate?" Ziko asked.

She toyed with her silverware. "I suppose it would make more sense to work together."

"I supposed it would."

"Although I'm not sure what good finding out who forged the drawing is going to do. It still passed DesignCorp's test."

"Did it?"

"I've got the test results."

"Do you?"

"Stop being so mysterious. What are you trying to say?"

"I've had time to think since I saw Mr. Kernfelter. I don't see how the altered design could pass the test. My design was carefully crafted to exert stressors and weight outwards to the brick walls. I thought out every angle and considered certain rules of physics when I designed it. If one dimension changed on my drawing, it would have changed the disposition of weight. Do you know what would happen then?"

"The third floor would collapse," she said.

"Yes. Where the third floor met the open atrium, where it appeared to defy gravity, that was a point of vulnerability. It couldn't be changed, not for any reason."

The waiter brought their food, quietly sliding the steaming dishes to the table in front of them.

When the waiter left, she pounced. "Who knew about the point of vulnerability?"

"No one. I never thought anyone would change my drawing, so I never told anyone. Well, except *Architectural Review* when I submitted my design for their award for emerging architecture."

"Your partner didn't know?"

"No. I didn't think I needed to tell anybody. DesignCorp tested it and it passed. That stamp of approval was good enough for me."

"So the only people who could have intended the Densmore to collapse were the staff at *Architectural Review* and anyone bright enough to figure out how your design worked."

Ziko scoffed. "I would have won an award for innovative design had the building not collapsed. Very few people could have figured out how it worked."

"Wait a minute, did you fill out the award application yourself or did someone help you?"

"I filled it out myself." Then he looked chagrined. "My secretary, Brittany Franks, typed it, but she doesn't have any architectural aptitude that I know of."

"But she works for an architectural firm."

"As a secretary."

Gabrielle gave him a condescending look. "I think secretaries understand more than you give them credit for, especially if they've worked in a field long enough."

Ziko shook his head. "Brittany's been with us less than a year, and I don't think she'd change the drawing. What reason would she have to?"

"That's what we need to find out—who changed the drawing and why."

"And whether the drawing really passed the test or not. I'm betting no."

That would mean the test was forged, too. She'd wondered why it looked hand-typed. Maybe it was. What did all this mean? She chewed the delicious moo goo gai pan while she thought.

"How is your firm financially?" she asked.

Ziko stirred a fork through his chop suey. "I'm not sure. Roger's been running the company while I was…away."

"We're going to need to see a current balance sheet and bank account statements."

"You think Roger had a hand in it? The drawing isn't Roger's work."

"Maybe he didn't do it alone, Mr. Ziko."

"You're talking about a conspiracy between my partner and someone else at my firm? And my name's Christian. My partner calls me by my childhood nickname, Kit, because that's how long he's known me and I've known him. He's my brother's best friend. You think with that kind of history between us he'd betray me?"

Obviously no one of importance had yet betrayed Christian. But if someone had, he'd learn.

"We have to investigate your partner the same as everyone else who could have done the forgery." She held up her hand when he would have spoken. "If only to rule him out."

His black brows drew together in thought as he spooned more rice onto his plate. "I suppose we have to work the investigation that way."

"Yes." She took a deep breath, reached down for the file on the seat next to her and held it out to him. "Here's the information you need."

He took the manila folder, his face solemn, his blue eyes darkened with some thought she couldn't read. "Thanks. I know what this cost you."

"No, you don't." She hated the almost bitter edge to her words, but she couldn't shake the fear that even handing him the file was jeopardizing a possible promotion. What if they fired her for actually investigating with Ziko? The insurance community was insular, almost inbred. Everybody knew everybody, either by name, reputation, or company. She had too many years experience to want to change professions now.

But her conscience wouldn't allow her to sleep at night if she didn't give this new investigation the same thoroughness she'd given the first part of it. How could she blithely pay her mother's bills with what would amount to blood money?

"Well, I appreciate what you're doing anyway." Christian moved his plate aside and paged through the file. "Here's one subcontractor we can rule out. St. Claire Shores Contracting was the primary builder for the project. That's my brother's company."

Damn. She had to disillusion him once more. She pushed her plate away, her appetite suddenly gone. "He can't be exempt because he's your brother for the same reason your partner isn't exempt."

Christian's face reddened. "I'd trust him with my life."

"That's not proof."

"How could I justify to Paul that I'm investigating him?"

"Then I'll investigate him. You won't have to."

His jaw muscles bunched. "I'm telling you he didn't do it."

"Are you going to fight me on every suspect? Take off those rose-colored glasses and think for a moment that someone may have even tried to frame you."

"Jesus, what world do you live in that you'd jump to that conclusion?"

His comment stung. It wasn't out of the realm of possibility, not if a desperate person wanted to hide his or her culpability by deflecting suspicion onto Christian. She wasn't jaded or anything like he hinted.

"I live in this world, Mr. Ziko. The one that put you in a jail cell yesterday."

He flinched. Good. She didn't want to be the only one being hit by barbs.

She had to pull herself together. She'd never felt such antagonism toward someone she hardly knew. Nor had anyone been able to wound her with words the way he had. Clearly, she needed to keep her distance from him.

"Why don't I do the investigation by myself? I won't be squeamish about interviewing your partner and your brother. After all, I'm a disinterested third party—"

"Not disinterested," he interrupted.

"Neutral party—" she continued, only to be interrupted again by his scoff. She bulled onward anyway. "I'll be able to get at the truth without emotions interfering."

"Are you like this all the time?" he asked.

"Like what?"

"Unfeeling?"

CHAPTER 7

Christian watched Gabrielle flinch from his harsh words, then her blue eyes narrowed and a bristly sort of armor rose up around her. Whether she did it to protect herself from hurt or to keep him out, he didn't know. But it made him sad. He'd never met anyone whose first instinct was to assume others would do bad things. Had someone hurt her so now she was wary like an animal that'd been beaten?

How could she live in this world without hope and trust? He had firm foundations of trust in Roger and Paul. Didn't she have anyone who loved her like Paul loved him?

He'd like to get to know her better. She was pretty, vibrant, and intelligent. What red-blooded man wouldn't want to get personal with her? But with this indictment hanging over his head the timing was terrible for any kind of involvement. For now, he'd have to stick to a professional relationship with her. And that meant not letting her investigate alone.

"I'm going with you when you talk to my brother and my partner. I want to see your face when you learn I'm right about them."

"Fine. We'll try your office first, talk to your partner and the other employees."

After agreeing to meet outside his office building in Troy, Gabrielle excused herself to call her office.

Christian wondered what she needed privacy to discuss. Then he was irritated with himself for wanting to know everything she said and did. Even though her blue eyes warmed with feminine interest when she looked at him, she did nothing to give him the go-ahead. In fact, she seemed to find his proximity disturbing.

Why did he continue to be attracted to a woman who didn't want him?

Maybe it was the desire to see her smile. Maybe he thought he could give her some hope to fan the flames of optimism in her. Or maybe he recognized a wounded spirit when he saw one and wanted to make things better.

At his office, Gabrielle parked next to him and came around to his door, scrutinizing his face. "You don't have to do this."

Christian wasn't sure he saw sympathy in her blue eyes. "I'm going to do it. I called Roger and told him I was coming to talk to him."

She nodded and walked beside him into the building. The silence was funereal. How did one go about doubting a friend and not feel this sickness in his stomach? Maybe people who didn't have a deep friendship like what he shared with Roger would feel nothing because they had nothing to lose. He surely did.

Gabrielle had affixed her plastic Michigan Casualty ID to her shirt. When they entered the offices of Barrett and Ziko, Brittany's gaze zoomed in on the ID and she frowned, pursing her full red lips.

"This is…" Christian began, only to be overridden by Gabrielle.

"Gabrielle Healey. I'm with Michigan Casualty, the firm that insured the Densmore. We have an appointment to see Roger Barrett."

Brittany glared at Christian, making him feel like a traitor. It was supposed to be Barrett and Ziko against all comers. He wasn't supposed to join the opposition.

"Just a minute and I'll tell him you're here."

She pushed the intercom. "Roger, Christian's here, and he's brought someone from Michigan Casualty with him." There was definite accusation in her voice.

After a pregnant pause, Roger's voice came through the intercom. "Send them back."

Christian led the way to Roger's office and held the door so Gabrielle could precede him inside. Roger's expression was confused, wary and accusatory, all at the same time.

Gabrielle approached his desk, identified herself and held out her hand.

Roger shook her hand, looking from her to Christian. "Kit, you didn't say you were bringing someone with you." His tone was accusatory.

"Something's come up, Roger." He might just as well spit it out. "Someone forged my signature on the revised drawing of the Densmore."

"Forged your signature?" Roger's frown turned to incredulous disbelief. "It can't be. I saw it. It's your signature."

"No, it's not. I took it to a handwriting expert this morning. He says someone else signed it."

"Was this guy a quack? Is he trying to put us out of business? And why did you take it to him anyway?"

Gabrielle interceded. "I sent Christian to him. And he's no quack. He's a certified expert who testifies regularly in court. He's going to give a deposition about the signature on the drawing."

Roger sank into his seat and ran a hand through his thinning hair. "Jesus. No one here would do such a thing. I thought you did the revision, Kit."

Had everyone thought he was guilty? "No. I knew I hadn't drawn it and I didn't remember signing off on it. It doesn't look like your work, either."

"I told Brittany to have you revise it. I assumed you'd done it."

"Why did you want it revised?"

Roger glanced at Gabrielle. "I'd prefer to tell you in private. This is business."

Gabrielle lifted her chin. "If it's related to the Densmore collapse, it's not business. It's evidence."

Roger rubbed the side of his face. His shoulders slumped. "We couldn't get the materials to meet the drawing specs."

"What do you mean?" Christian said. "I'm not aware of any material shortage."

"The thirty-foot girders. Kit, we couldn't get them. When we placed our order, the price had tripled. We couldn't afford them."

Christian couldn't believe it. "We could have cut corners someplace else. We had to have those girders."

"No. Paul tried every way he could work it. The length had to be shorter."

"Jesus, Roger, the design doesn't work at any other length. We could have decreased our profit margin or something to absorb the price increase."

Roger slammed his fist onto the desk. "Dammit, Kit, we couldn't."

Christian got a cold feeling in the pit of his stomach. Something was going on in their business, something he should have been aware of. "What aren't you telling me?"

"This isn't for outside ears." Roger turned to Gabrielle. "And it isn't related to the Densmore, either."

For a moment, Gabrielle looked mulish, like she'd demand to stay and hear what Roger had to say.

"Would you mind giving us a minute?" Christian needed to know what was happening at his company.

"All right." She turned and walked out, closing the door behind her.

"Okay, spill," Christian said.

Roger rose to his feet. "How dare you bring her here. You're a partner in this firm. Your first interest is the firm."

Stung and feeling guilt over neglecting the business, Christian's reply was sharper than it should have been. "My first interest is in staying out of jail, but I seem to be the only one concerned with that."

Roger scrubbed his face. He looked old and tired all of a sudden. "I'm sorry, Kit. I've been so busy trying to hold our heads above water, I haven't had time for your problems. We've got so many projects happening at once and not enough hands here to help. I had to send Jeremy out to the West Park jobsite."

That news shocked Christian. Roger's son wasn't that good yet. "Jeremy's not ready for that."

"What else was I supposed to do? We've got commitments to meet. I've covered as many as I can, but I'm only one man."

Christian was drowning in guilt. He should have been able to handle life's ups and downs, not fallen apart like some child. Roger hadn't gone into a decline. No, his partner had been strong and done more than his share of the work.

Christian thrust his shoulders back and lifted his chin. He was here now. "I'm sorry I let you down. What do you need me to do?"

"I need you to carry a partner's share of the load. I need you to take the heat off our company. I need you to make the damn rain stop long enough so at least one of our projects can come in on time and at budget. I need you to convince me what you're doing now isn't part of some psychosis you're experiencing that means you'll be back in Crittenden within the week. And I need to know why you brought that damn woman here."

His partner had been under too much strain for too long. Christian tried to give him the answers he deserved. "I can't control the rain, but you'll have to tell me how badly the weather is hurting us financially."

"It's bad. Every project in process is late, so payments to us are late. Foundations are late because the ground is a soaking mud pit. We can't keep the concrete dry. We're spending extra money on pumps to empty water out of foundations. The wood's in danger of getting warped. We've already had to replace some of the boards at the Water Towne project. God, was that one aptly named. And we have to pay a thousand bucks a day fine on the government building on Pinewood for every day we're past the deadline. We're already a week overdue."

"And that's what you didn't want Gabrielle to hear?"

"Damn right. I don't need word spread all over town that we can't pay our bills or meet our commitments."

"I don't think Gabrielle would tell anyone that."

Roger glared at him. "She's out to pin the Densmore disaster on us."

"She's trying to help me find out who forged my name on the drawing."

"Then what the hell is she doing here?"

Christian rubbed the back of his neck. "It could have been someone who works or worked here."

"We've got five employees, Kit. If you didn't do it, that leaves four, including me. Don't tell me you suspect me?" His voice rose at the end.

"We'd better let Gabrielle back in if we're going to talk about this." Christian moved to the door, but Roger's next words stopped him.

"Jesus, you believe it could have been me?"

Christian's face heated with shame and guilt. As much as he wanted this discussion to be private between Roger and him, Gabrielle needed to hear it. He opened the door to her.

She stepped through, looking from him to Roger. Then she quietly closed the door.

"Do you suspect me, too?" Roger pointed at her.

"I need to rule out everyone to find the guilty one. Did you forge Christian's name on the drawing?"

"Jesus Christ, I can't believe this. You're my goddamned partner. I invited you into my business and this is the way you repay me? Your brother's my best friend. What's the matter with you? Did those drugs fry your brain?"

Roger stalked back and forth behind his desk. "I took you into my business because your brother asked me to. I taught you the ropes. I made a place for you when you graduated because you added something to this company it didn't have before. I can't believe you'd accuse me."

It was worse than Christian had imagined watching trust fracture. He could never call back the words, nor make Roger forget he'd heard them. He felt helpless to ease Roger's pain, but he was angry, too. He'd sweated as much blood for this firm as Roger had, yet Roger made him sound like a green intern instead of a partner.

Gabrielle spoke before he could say something else to Roger he'd regret. "You didn't answer my question."

"You go to hell."

"If Christian Ziko is such an integral part of your business, why won't you assure him you didn't forge his name?"

"I didn't forge his name." Roger growled through his perfect white teeth.

Christian let out his breath in relief.

"Then you'll submit a sample of your handwriting for analysis?" Gabrielle asked.

"Yes." Roger glared daggers at her.

"Thank you. If you'd sign your name several times on one side of a piece of paper and write Christian's name on the other side, I'll present them to the handwriting expert later today."

Roger dropped into his desk chair, snatched a sheet of paper from his drawer and proceeded to write violently on it. The pen scratched sharply enough that Christian wondered why it didn't tear right through the paper.

Neither Christian nor Gabrielle said anything while Roger filled the sheet with handwriting. His face got redder when he had to write Christian's name. When he finished, he thrust the page at Gabrielle.

"Thank you. I need to ask the same question of all your other employees, and I need the contact information of the intern who worked here when the Densmore was being built."

Roger opened a file drawer and pulled out a number of manila file folders. "Here are all the interns for the past two years. Now I've got work to do, since my business partner is otherwise occupied."

It was a direct hit to Christian's solar plexus. But he'd pull his weight. "Give me a copy of the most recent financials so I can get back up to speed. And if there's something you can hand off to me today, give me that as well."

Roger glared at him for a moment, then pulled another folder from his drawer and handed it to Christian. He grabbed a stack of papers and drawings from the corner of his desk and shoved them into Christian's arms without a word.

Christian tried to offer his partner some hope. "I'll be back to work full-time as soon as we find out who forged my name."

"If there's a business to get back to."

Christian took the hurt as his due. How would he feel if Roger accused him of something like this? He'd lash out in pain, too.

When they were in the corridor with a door between them and Roger, Gabrielle spoke. "I'm sorry. We had to rule him out."

He took his frustration out on her. "Yeah. He's only the man I own a business with. Who needs trust with him?"

CHAPTER 8

Christian stalked away from the scene in Roger's office and Gabrielle sighed. She felt like she'd kicked a puppy.

His secretary narrowed her eyes when she saw him. "Roger's never raised his voice to you before. What's going on and what has she got to do with it?" She pointed at Gabrielle.

There was a hard look in the secretary's eyes incongruent with her bimbo figure. There was more to this woman than most people would guess. Of course, most men wouldn't look past the triple E-sized chest.

"We need to talk to you away from the front desk," Christian said. "Please come into my office."

The secretary sashayed down the hall. Her skirt and blouse were tight, displaying her feminine assets quite well. A woman like Brittany could easily capture any man's attention. Gabrielle disliked her on sight. She hated that Brittany worked with Christian, which made no sense at all.

Christian's office was a direct contrast to Roger's. Where Roger's desk, tables and file cabinets had been covered with folders, drawings, papers and what looked like Lego sets, Christian's office was pristine, as though he hadn't been here in awhile. The only thing out of place was a blueprint tube with a letter attached to it on top of his desk.

Christian ran his fingertips across the glossy wooden desktop. When he glanced at the letter attached to the cardboard tube, his lips flattened. Then he looked up at his secretary.

"Brittany, someone signed my name on the revised Densmore drawing. As much as it pains me to ask, I need to know if you did it."

"What? Did Roger put you up to this?"

"No. Did you have anything to do with forging my signature?"

"No, I didn't. And if you or Roger try to pin that on me in order to fire me, I'll sue so fast your heads will spin."

"Why do you think either partner would want to fire you?" Gabrielle asked. Something about Brittany's reaction was odd.

Brittany licked her lips in a suggestive manner. "Why do you think they'd want to fire me?"

Message received loud and clear, whether it was the truth or not. Was Brittany sleeping with either or both partners and now one or both of them were done with her and it was awkward to see her at work every day?

"We need samples of your handwriting to confirm your innocence." Gabrielle gave the same instructions she'd given Roger.

Brittany slanted Gabrielle a deprecating glance before she sidled around Christian's desk and eased herself into his chair, making it a sensual act between her and the leather seat. Then she began to write.

Christian wandered the office, touching things with his fingertips. His manner was possessive, but sadness surrounded him. Once again, his vulnerability tried to pull Gabrielle in.

"There." Brittany thrust the paper toward Gabrielle.

Gabrielle took it and intentionally touched Brittany's hand during the exchange. She wasn't prepared for the graphic vision that filled her mind.

A naked man with black hair was hunched over Brittany having torrid sex with her. From the edge of the bed where he stood, he pulled her kneeling body into his desperate thrusts with a lusty grip on her large breasts. Her head was thrown back against his in passion, her hair hiding his face.

Gabrielle tore her hand away. She didn't want to see any more of Brittany and the man she thought was Christian. She tasted bile in her throat and thought she'd be sick at the idea of the two of them together. Worse, she thought less of Christian for giving in to his base needs with a woman like Brittany. Someone like him who dreamed of innovation should want something different, not something every other man lusted after.

"Is that all?" Brittany's tone was businesslike to Christian, but her glance at Gabrielle was cold.

"Yes, thanks, Brittany," Christian said.

Was that residual warmth in his voice toward his former lover, Gabrielle wondered? A woman scorned had an excellent motive for revenge.

"I'll go get Jeremy Barrett," Christian said to Gabrielle. "Roger's son joined the firm last year."

As soon as Gabrielle was alone, she took the opportunity to look over his things so she could learn more about the man. There were two awards for design on the bookshelf. The books were an eclectic mix of designs of buildings, gardens, houses, bridges and other structures. She paused at a couple of books about physics. He'd said the Densmore plan had been based on physics theories.

Pulling one book free, she thumbed through it. There were post-it notes tacked to several pages. The first bookmarked section dealt with opposing forces, and she remembered Christian talking about resisting gravity. He truly had researched his ideas, not just drawn something that looked innovative.

As she flipped to the next marked section, a piece of paper slipped out and floated to the floor. It was a note on DesignCorp letterhead:

Kit,
It sounds right to me.
J

A picture formed in her mind. *A thirtyish man with dark hair and glasses stood with Christian in front of a remote control. Both men wore goggles.*

"Ready?" the man name J asked.

"Yeah," Christian said.

There was a small explosion and a rocket lifted into the air not far from them. Both men whooped. As the vision faded, Gabrielle smiled.

Christian had a friend at DesignCorp close enough to call him by his nickname. Even his secretary, someone who might have been his lover, called him by his legal name.

"What's that?" Christian asked from right behind her.

She jerked in surprise and guilt that she'd been contemplating his love life again. She handed him the paper. "This was in your book."

"Oh. It's nothing."

"Who's J?" she asked.

"Jake Patoni. He's a friend of mine."

"I can tell by how he addressed you. Do you normally bounce ideas off him?"

"Only when they're radical. It saves our company time and money if the designs are feasible up front. I met him at U of M when I was there. He's an engineer."

"So you spend time with him during your off hours?"

"Yeah. Jeremy isn't here. He's out at the West Park site." He frowned at something. "We'll either have to try to catch him there or at another time." He looked at his watch. "I've got to be at my lawyer's office at two. That's on the opposite end of town from the West Park site, so I can't hit one before I have to be at the other."

"I'll go see Jeremy, then your brother."

"I want to be there when you talk to Paul."

"I want to see as many people this afternoon as possible. I can't wait for you to finish with your lawyer. Who knows how many hours you'll be tied up."

"You could see the other subcontractors on the list."

"Christian, it makes more sense to visit the suspects in the order of importance. The closer a suspect is to the job, the more motive he or she would have to forge the drawing."

"Please, Gabrielle. I need to be there."

Sighing, she gave in. "Fine. But call me the minute you're finished with your lawyer."

"I'll do that."

"You want to give me the intern's name and contact information so I can track him down?"

"Sure. Give me a couple of minutes to figure out the timeframe and go through the files."

As Christian sat down in his black leather chair and pulled the personnel files Roger had given him toward him, Gabrielle returned to her interrupted study of his office.

The framed prints on the wall were spectacular views of famous suspension bridges. She wondered if he'd wanted to build bridges instead of buildings. It was a limited field, so maybe he'd thought his job prospects were better in commercial construction.

But her instincts said he'd stayed close to his family. She knew his parents were dead and Paul was his only sibling. Christian worked with Paul's best friend. Yes, he'd tied himself closely to his brother's life. There was nothing wrong with that, but a man as arrogant in his profession as Christian Ziko could create on a grander scale if he left home. The inconsistency about Ziko peaked her curiosity.

"Here you go." Christian held out a piece of paper to her. "I'm sorry, but it could have been one of two interns during that timeframe. I couldn't pin it down any tighter."

"It's not a problem. I'll investigate both of them."

As they walked past Brittany's desk, the woman just nodded. But Gabrielle noted the secretary's gaze was still on them as she passed through the outer door. Was it personal or professional interest, she wondered?

They went to their separate cars, to go their separate ways, her to build a case against a suspect, him to build a defense for himself. She was sure each was equally determined to succeed. But did each have as much to lose if they didn't?

CHAPTER 9

Attorney Bryce Gannon was a cold, emotionless man whose blue eyes could hypnotize prey with their piercing intensity. Christian had always thought blond was a warm hair color, but not on Bryce. He'd removed his suit jacket and the shirt underneath was blinding white and starched to perfection. He was in his late thirties or early forties and well preserved.

Why would Paul be friends with a man like this?

"You look a lot like your brother." Bryce gestured to a maroon leather chair in front of his desk.

Christian hadn't expected to hear anything personal from this impersonal man. He sat stiffly in the chair, uncomfortable to be here. "Paul said you could help me."

"He told me about the grand jury indictment and what happened at the Densmore. Why don't you give me your side of the story?"

Immediately Christian felt antagonistic toward the attorney. He'd battled Paul and Roger's doubts, and now it appeared Bryce was infected with them as well.

He rose to his feet. "I don't know how you got the impression I might be guilty, but I'm not. There's no 'side' to the story. I'm innocent and I have nothing to hide. Period."

Bryce held up a hand. "Hold on, Christian. I never said I thought you were guilty, but your brother inferred you may have made a mistake on the drawing which led to the collapse."

Christian's fists clenched. "That's a goddamned lie. That drawing was altered by someone else who forged my signature."

The look of cynical forbearance on the lawyer's face infuriated Christian.

"Christian, Paul told me what Sean Bergman said about your mental state. This sounds like paranoid delusion to me."

Damn their fraternity. Apparently even Paul couldn't be trusted with HIPAA access. Christian was never going to use another one of Paul's frat brothers again. "We're through here." Christian turned to leave.

"Wait a minute. What did I say to upset you?"

Christian continued toward the office door. "I'm sure the American Bar Association will recommend another attorney. Oh, by the way, if Alex Kernfelter calls, tell him you're no longer on my case."

As Christian opened the door, a powerful opposing force slammed it shut.

Bryce was right behind him, his eyes blue flames. There wasn't anything cold about him now. "Your brother asked me to defend you, and I'm damn well going to do that." It was practically a snarl.

"Get your hand off the damned door."

"What did Alex Kernfelter have to say?" Bryce asked.

Christian yanked the door partially open. "Not that it's any of your business since you're not defending me, but he's going to testify that it's not my signature on the blueprint."

Bryce released his hold on the door. "Sit down, Christian." His voice was calm and controlled once more.

"I don't think so."

"Listen, I owe your brother this. Come hell or high water, I'm going to defend you to the best of my ability, which is a lot in this town."

"I'd rather you defend me because I'm innocent, not because you owe my brother a debt." What kind of debt could Bryce possibly have incurred from Paul?

"If Kernfelter's going to testify in your defense, that's a good enough endorsement of your innocence for me."

Christian crossed his arms on his chest. "But my word's not enough."

Bryce sighed. "I've worked with so many guilty people recently, I've begun to assume everyone's guilty. I'm sorry."

Gabrielle was the same way. Some of the righteous indignation left Christian, but not all of it. "Listen, I'll tell Paul we weren't a good fit. He won't blame you for not taking my case."

"We just got off on the wrong foot. I'm sorry about that. We can start over."

Christian shook his head. How could he explain what he needed? "I don't think you'll understand what I'm about to say, but it's important to me. No one believes in me. That's never happened to me before. Paul thinks I made a mistake. Roger thought I'd redone the drawing. Paul and Roger are the two most important people in my life, but right now I can't count on either of them. I don't like how it makes me feel, like I'm all alone.

"Gabrielle Healey, from Michigan Casualty, is helping me try to find the forger, but she's not doing it for my benefit. As long as somebody's guilty, her company doesn't have to pay.

"You mentioned my mental state. People don't understand bipolar. They think I'm insane and that I can't tell truth from fiction. I have to hide the fact I was committed, so even when I tell the truth, I'm lying.

"Last month I was on top of the world. Today people want to spit on me. I need someone to believe in me, to prove to me and everyone else I didn't make a mistake horrible enough to cause the deaths of six people. Then I can begin to believe in myself again."

Christian stopped, taken aback by the echo of the words in his head. He hadn't known all that was festering inside him.

"I understand," Bryce said, without elaboration. "Sit down and let's begin. Tell me about Kernfelter and this investigation. The faster we find the guilty party, the faster we can get the charges against you dropped."

Bryce sounded so convincing Christian almost believed it would be that simple. He wanted and needed to believe he could rebuild his life again.

So he returned to his seat and told Bryce everything that had happened so far. To his credit, the lawyer listened with an impassive face to every word, only interrupting to clarify some point.

"Why didn't you go to the police?" Bryce asked.

Christian leaned forward. "Do you really think they'd do a thorough job in a timely manner? I don't. I've got a vested interest in clearing my name as soon as possible."

"But you're not a trained investigator."

"Gabrielle Healey is."

"I don't think it's wise for you to work with her."

Christian frowned. "Why not?"

"For one thing, it's a conflict of interest on her part. For another, you should be looking out for your and Roger's corporate interests. I'm not asking you to hide the guilty party, if it's someone in your firm," Bryce said. "I just don't want Michigan Casualty to be privy to whatever information you find that might reflect badly on Barrett and Ziko. What good will it be if you're cleared, if you lose your company? As your attorney, I advise you to protect your personal and professional welfare, if it's possible."

The thought that Barrett and Ziko could be fatally hurt if one of their employees was the culprit had not occurred to Christian. But if the firm was tainted, neither he nor Roger might be able to rise above that.

"You mean separate the guilt of the individual from the guilt of the firm for employing that person?"

"Something like that."

"How do you sleep at night?"

Bryce's blue eyes became glacial. "Because I have friends like Roger and Paul. Even if you don't want to protect Roger's business interests, I do."

What the hell went on at that fraternity that first Bryce owed Paul and now it seemed he owed Roger something as well?

"I'm very interested in the health of my company." Guilt stabbed him yet again, for hadn't Roger told him less than an hour ago Barrett and Ziko was being hard-pressed?

"Then stay away from Ms. Healey. We'll do our own investigation."

"She's not going to stop just because I'm not with her. And if she interviews people first, they may not talk to me later."

Bryce sighed and tossed his gold pen onto the desktop. "You're being difficult."

"I'm sorry, but I told you my reasons up front." Christian shrugged. "At least I know Gabrielle's agenda. I have no illusions about her."

"Forewarned is forearmed, I suppose. Just don't air any dirty laundry in front of her. And if you find out anything not pertinent to her investigation, don't share it."

Christian sighed. Would nothing ever be clear-cut again? Sure, he'd hidden being bipolar for years, but now there would be other things to hide. Maybe this was the point called adulthood, where one's life wasn't an open book to everyone who wanted to read it. Maybe Paul had protected Christian far beyond the point when other people stood on their own two feet and knew adult expectations. And maybe Christian had let him.

"I'll do my best."

"I'll file a motion to dismiss based on the forgery and see where that goes."

*

Gabrielle decided she didn't like Jeremy Barrett even before she shook his hand. Where his father, with a distinguished career, had a reason for his confidence, Jeremy was just an arrogant bastard.

She heard him yelling from twenty yards away as she picked her way carefully through the skeleton of the West Park construction.

"No, no, no. Dammit, can't you read a blueprint?" Jeremy's voice was higher than Roger's.

When she caught sight of him, she knew immediately he was Roger's son by his thin blondish hair. But the twenty-something Jeremy carried more weight than he should, making him appear like an ill-formed copy of Roger.

A hard-hatted construction worker stormed away from Jeremy, red-faced and stiff-backed. Jeremy's light blue eyes, another gift from Roger, flicked over her, noted her ID badge and then returned to the blueprint laid on the board in front of him.

"Jeremy Barrett?"

"Yeah." He looked up. "What can I do for you?"

"Gabrielle Healey from Michigan Casualty. I'm investigating the Densmore Building collapse. I need to ask you a few questions." She held out her hand.

When he took it and gave a quick shake with a limp hand, a vision filled her mind.

Jeremy had his back pressed against the wall of what looked like a corridor at Barrett and Ziko Architectural. Although his face was red, he looked like he might cry. He pushed away from the wall and stormed down the hall, entering an office and closing the door.

"It was all a damn lie. He doesn't want me here. He doesn't want to spend time with me. He won't give me any responsibility. He gives all the good projects to Ziko. He's a bastard, just like Mom said. But I'll make him see he's wrong about me."

The vision dispersed. Jeremy looked away toward the men and women moving around with the purpose of worker bees. "I didn't work on the Densmore. That was Christian Ziko's baby." He didn't manage to hide the hard edge in his voice.

"Something has come to light. If you'd please give me a few minutes in private, I can complete my business with you."

"Whatever business you have should be with Ziko."

"This is specific to you."

He frowned, pushing out his lower lip so he appeared petulant. "I don't know how it could be." Looking at her set face, he blew out a breath. "All right, you've got five minutes."

Heading back to the parking lot, Gabrielle wondered if even the blunt approach would work with Jeremy. If he wanted to lie, he would. How could Christian bear to work with him? She thought it very telling that Jeremy didn't call Christian Kit.

When Jeremy reached the area where the workers' pick-ups and SUVs were parked, he turned, crossed his arms across his chest, and asked, "What do you have to say to me?"

She thought she'd shock a reaction out of him. "Did you forge Christian Ziko's signature on the revised Densmore blueprint?"

Jeremy's eyes widened for a moment, then they narrowed. "You dragged me over her to make accusations against me? Who sent you, Ziko?"

"My company sent me, the company that insured the Densmore for millions of dollars. Did you forge Ziko's signature?"

"He did the drawing himself. Nobody forged his signature."

"No, he didn't do the second drawing, and he didn't sign it, either. I'm going to need a sample of your handwriting."

"Not likely. You're trying to pin this on me instead of Daddy's favorite. Well, I'm not going to play. If Ziko messed up, he should pay for it."

Oh, he was a crafty one. There was just enough honest indignation to make her want to believe something he said was true. But which part of his statement was the lie?

"You're going to have to give the court a sample of your handwriting, so you might as well give it to me now."

"It's going to take a court order to make me write anything. I know my rights. I don't have to incriminate myself, since I already know somebody's going to pull something and get the results to point at me. No way."

"Do you think your father would let anyone do that to you?"

"My dad doesn't give a crap about me. His wife and girlfriends are all he thinks about. Oh, and his business. And now politics."

Interesting. This might explain why Christian hadn't gotten close to Jeremy. "Your dad hired you."

"He wanted a Barrett at Barrett and Ziko when he ran for office. It looks good to the voting public. Believe me, it's not personal."

"What can I do to convince you the handwriting expert is completely impartial and won't be swayed by anyone to fix the results?"

"Not a damn thing. I hope Ziko gets what he deserves."

Gabrielle controlled her anger on Christian's behalf. It wouldn't do to show emotions to this young man. "Then I'm sorry I wasted both our time. I'm sure you'll be subpoenaed by the court, so you'd better put a lawyer on retainer."

Then she turned and walked away toward her car. She didn't take an easy breath until she was down the street from the construction site and could pull to the curb without being seen. Jeremy Barrett had issues with his father and Christian. He seethed with righteous anger, but he acted like a spoiled, sulky child. He had motive and opportunity, but was he all hot air, or had he taken action?

She called Christian and reported her conversation with Jeremy.

Christian was silent for a few moments after she finished. "I think you misread the situation."

"No, Christian, I didn't." She tried to rein in her temper. "I don't want to discuss this over the phone. Are you ready to see your brother?"

"Yeah. I'll call him and see where he's at, then call you back." He broke the connection.

Christian didn't want to believe the people closest to him would hurt him. It was his point of vulnerability, like a blind spot.

He called back to report Paul was at a job site in Warren, gave her directions and agreed to wait for her to arrive before he questioned his brother.

As she parked beside Christian's Jeep in a steady rain, the overhead light came on in his car. There was another man sitting in the front seat next to him.

Gabrielle stepped gingerly out into the mud and her foot sank in nearly to the top of her shoes. She was soaked by the time she closed the Jeep's door.

"You made good time considering," Christian said.

"I've got permanent cricks in my hands from gripping the wheel." She turned to the other man.

Paul Ziko looked a lot like Christian, in a nagging familiar way— the same jet-black hair and the same Caribbean blue eyes. Only where Christian's face was intense, Paul's looked approachable, an any-man face. There were smile lines at the corners of his eyes and mouth, but he wasn't smiling now. Rain like they'd had all spring was probably a contractor's worst nightmare.

His blue eyes assessed her warily.

She reached her hand between the bucket seats to shake his. "I'm Gabrielle Healey from Michigan Casualty."

When he touched her, she got a vision, but it wasn't the one she expected.

Paul talked into a phone receiver he held in a white knuckled grip. "Pam, please, I'm sorry."

"It's too late for sorry. You know better than to call me. You're supposed to talk to my lawyer."

"I want you back. I made a mistake."

"Yeah, you did."

"Let me make it up to you, Pam. Let me make it right."

"It's never going to be right again. Stop calling me, Paul." The connection was severed.

Paul picked up a tumbler of golden liquid, tossed down a healthy gulp and then held the glass to his cheek. He still gripped the phone in the other hand. A tear slipped down his face.

"I'm sorry," he whispered.

Gabrielle released Paul's hand and the vision. It was too personal, and made her wonder what he was guilty of. With a woman on the other end of the phone, one he wanted back, she assumed it was his wife.

He turned to say something to Christian, and when he did the sense of familiarity coalesced into something else. She'd seen his profile before, in a vision with Brittany Franks, Christian's secretary. They'd been having frantic sex. Now the vision made more sense. His marriage had crumbled as a result.

"What's wrong, Gabrielle?" Christian asked.

Paul was the main contractor on the Densmore. He'd been having an affair with the architect's secretary. His wife had found out. Could his personal catastrophe have started a string of errors that led to forgery and disaster? Maybe if she rattled him first, he'd admit he'd made a mistake.

"When does your divorce become final, Mr. Ziko?"

Paul's head snapped around, his blue eyes wide and startled. "Where'd you hear that?"

"Court filings are public record," she said, although it wasn't how she'd found out.

"What do you want?"

"Did you forge Christian's name on the revised Densmore drawing?"

"What? That's crazy, that's..." His face reddened and he straightened. "That's a damned lie."

"If it's a lie, you want to explain how your affair with Brittany Franks affected the Densmore construction?"

CHAPTER 10

Christian couldn't believe it. But guilt was written in every strained line of his brother's face.

"My God." It was only a breath of sound. "You had an affair with Brittany?" Christian felt betrayed. That was why Pam had filed for divorce. It made sense now.

"Kit, it's not true…" Paul's protest petered off.

"You told me you and Pam were getting divorced because you didn't spend enough time together. You lied to me."

"I made a mistake."

"A mistake is ordering the wrong color of paint. You're happily married, or you were."

"I was lonely. Pam was never at home. She'd joined all those charities, so she was out every night. Then one evening Brittany's car needed a tow, and it was raining, so I gave her a ride home."

"And another kind of ride." Christian had believed Paul was a tower of strength, a man of steel. Now what was he?

"It just…happened. I didn't plan it."

"You must have been thinking about it," Christian said. "Probably every time you came to the office."

"I'm married, not dead. I look at pretty women, especially when they're built like Brittany."

"But you did more than look, and now Pam's divorcing you."

"I made a mistake. Who are you to judge me? Look at the mistake you made."

Christian sucked in his breath. The accusation hurt terribly. He'd known his brother doubted him, but to hear that doubt voiced aloud made it doubly painful.

"I didn't," he said on a flare of heat.

"Christian didn't make a mistake." Gabrielle's voice came clearly from the back seat.

"What?" Paul's head whipped around again.

"Someone forged his signature to the altered drawing. Was it you, Paul?"

Paul's face slowly drained of color. "What are you accusing me of?"

"I can see why you might have done it. You were caught in an adulterous affair. Your wife lashed out. You fell apart. You had deadlines to meet, but the rain kept falling. Work fell behind schedule. You needed to make up the time somehow. Christian's design took a lot of care to build, time you didn't have. If you substituted shorter material, the building could go up a lot faster. There was just the tiny detail of the drawing. You already had his signature on the original. All you had to do was trace it. Did Brittany help you forge the test results?"

"I'd never do that, not to any architect and sure as hell not to my brother." He turned to Christian. "Kit, I'd never do that to you."

But Christian hadn't thought Paul would cheat on his wife or sleep with Brittany and cover it up. If he did those things…

"It's not true, Kit. I swear to God."

This was his brother, who'd held Christian as he cried for their dead parents. His brother who had found Kit nearly catatonic with depression and saved him, not once, but twice. Paul, who had protected Christian and smoothed the way for him, so he could have everything he'd ever dreamed of. Paul, who was his only family, his rock. His rock with a crack in it.

"You swear?" Christian was pitiful in his need to believe Paul was still Superman, still the Lone Ranger who came riding in to save the day. His brother had been his hero since his earliest memories. Christian needed him to be that hero again.

"I swear I didn't do it."

Christian swallowed and nodded. "I believe you." Then he had to bring up something equally painful. "But you believed I'd made a mistake on the Densmore drawing."

Paul looked away. "Yeah. I believed it. People make mistakes, even you." There was a bite of accusation in the last two words. Paul hadn't forgiven him.

"I wouldn't have made that kind of mistake, not with that design."

"You're human, Kit. Just because you believe your design is infallible doesn't mean it is. Just because the great Christian Ziko designed it, doesn't mean it's impervious to disaster. Things happen."

"It had help," Gabrielle said.

Paul glared at her. "What are you talking about?"

"Christian had the signature on the drawing analyzed by an expert who will testify in court it's not Christian's signature."

"My God, it's true?" Paul looked at Christian for confirmation.

"Yeah."

"And you're pointing fingers at everybody who had anything to do with the Densmore...or just at me because of Brittany? Did she accuse me, too?"

"No, she didn't say anything to us." Christian stared at Gabrielle, suddenly uneasy. How had she known about his brother and Brittany? His secretary hadn't said a word while he was in the room.

*

Gabrielle knew the moment Christian suspected her. His black eyebrows drew together. Wariness darkened his blue eyes to navy. She knew her secret was safe—no one's first thought was she was psychic. Even though she'd wanted him to take off his rose-colored glasses and not trust so freely, she didn't want his first reticence to be with her. She felt the loss of trust like an empty hole in her chest.

"You actually believed I'd hurt you like that?" Paul asked Christian.

"No. But we have to rule out everybody."

"She made you come here, didn't she?" Paul jerked his thumb toward Gabrielle.

Christian looked weary all of a sudden. "Yes."

Gabrielle reclaimed Paul's attention. "It's my job to find the guilty party, Mr. Ziko. Are you willing to submit handwriting samples for the expert to compare?"

Paul's sigh gusted out into the confines of the car. "Yes. Whatever it takes to prove to my brother I'd never do that to him. Since my love isn't enough to make him trust me."

Christian reached out to Paul, but Paul waved away his hand. "No. Don't try to make up for it just yet. I'm not ready."

"I didn't want this to come between us."

"How did you think it wouldn't?" Hurt coated Paul's words.

Gabrielle slid the tablet and a pen to Paul and told him what to do. Paul glared at her, then looked mulishly at his brother. But when he glanced down at the paper, Gabrielle caught the hurt he tried to hide.

Despite the difference in their ages, these two men shared a tight bond she envied. She hoped they could forgive each other and be close once more. She'd give anything for someone to love her the way they obviously loved one another. Even with Paul's doubts about Christian, Paul hadn't stopped loving him.

She couldn't resist one last touch when Paul handed her the tablet.

At first she thought the picture was blurred. But the sound of heaving breaths and the jolting scenery clued her to someone running.

"Hurry!" a young man's voice, tight with strain, yelled from ahead.

"Sean, look out," someone yelled.

A young man, about twenty, with mud-brown hair stumbled over a fallen log in the knee-high weeds. Another young man with thin blondish hair and light blue eyes grabbed the one named Sean's arm to steady him, then urged him to keep running. It was Roger Barrett, in his early twenties.

The lead runner looked back. In the near darkness, Gabrielle thought it was Christian. But his face was rounder. Paul.

"You guys gotta hurry. He's in trouble." His voice was nearly panicked.

The three young men broke through the weeds into the water of a lake, splashing loudly. There was a wooden cage of some kind sticking a few inches out of the water, and Paul Ziko dragged futilely at it. Sean and Roger helped him pull.

A knife in Roger's hand flashed in the moonlight. He dived into the water. A moment later, the crate bobbed to the surface. The sound of gasping came from within it.

"Get him out of there," Paul cried.

The three men dragged the cage off the fourth bedraggled man. Whatever color his hair was normally, was coated with muck. His eyebrows were dark blond. They pulled him out of the water and onto the flattened grass where he lay gasping.

"I told you," Paul said.

Roger knelt by the man, who was spitting out water. "What made you think they'd pledge you, Gannon?"

"I thought they were my friends," the young man gasped.

"They're not. They would have left you to die."

"They lied to me."

"We'd never do that to you," Paul said in a quiet voice.

The others nodded. The look in the downed man's eyes was eloquent as he grasped their offered hands.

Gabrielle slid her hand from Paul's. He opened the car door, letting in the moisture of the falling rain and the smell of damp earth.

"Paul…" Christian grabbed his brother's arm.

"Don't, Kit."

Christian let go and Paul left the car, slamming the door with a solid thud. He ran across the muddy lot to another vehicle and climbed in.

"I should hate you for what just happened," Christian said in a low voice.

Gabrielle's chest tightened. "You knew it had to be done. I told you not to come. It would have been better if you hadn't been here. Then your relationship with your brother would have remained intact."

He stared out the front windshield into the pouring rain. The windows were fogged from their breathing, but she didn't recommend turning on the defroster. He was a powder keg looking for a reason to explode.

"I've alienated the people I depend on most. I didn't know how much support I had until I lost it."

No platitudes would help him, so she didn't mouth any. But she wondered what would help. She hated the slump of his shoulders, the desolate blankness of his face, his white-knuckled grip on the steering wheel.

So she shared her own pain. "My mother is fifty-four years old. She had a massive stroke in December, right before the holidays, and was paralyzed on the right side. The doctors said she was lucky she didn't die. Even after months of therapy, she has trouble talking. She can't walk. She lives in a nursing home. I don't think she feels very lucky she lived, but I'm glad she did, because otherwise I'd be all alone."

"My parents are dead. Paul's all I have."

"I know. I'm sorry."

Christian turned to her. His blue eyes were bright with unshed tears. "I can't lose anything else."

Her heart went out to him. She had the strangest desire to hold him in her arms and stroke his hair back from his forehead. From almost the moment she'd first seen him, he'd evoked feelings in her she didn't expect or want. This man wasn't for her. But she felt like she was in tune with him, and she'd never felt that way with anyone else before.

"We'll find the forger and clear your name. Your brother and your partner will understand, and if necessary, forgive you for doubting. They both seem to be under a lot of stress right now."

"Yeah. Rain's bad for construction. I think it's bad for people's tempers, too."

Now that Christian seemed calmer, Gabrielle felt easier discussing the case. "I left a message for one of the interns, but I haven't had a chance to call the other one yet. Let me do that now."

She found out Bryan Tuckerman was about a mile from their present location and he agreed to meet with them. Before she could get out of Christian's Jeep, he spoke.

"Gabrielle?"

She hesitated, drawn as much by the quality of his voice as his unvoiced question.

"I don't hate you."

Gabrielle pondered the ramifications of his statement all the way to the next location. The rain stopped midway there, so she could spare her concentration from the road. No, she didn't want Christian to hate her. But she didn't want anything more from him, either. Liar, her conscience taunted her.

So she wanted to watch his face as he made his dreams come to life on paper. Her arms ached to give a loving harbor to someone, and Christian needed such a harbor. She needed someone to understand how alone she felt, and Christian would. He needed someone to believe in him. So did she. He needed to heal. So did she.

Gabrielle sighed. The thought tantalized that together they could heal one another. She'd never know if she didn't rise above her fear. But it almost choked her to think about being dumped again. It had been almost two years since the last dating fiasco that had soured her on men. Maybe she should have tried again sooner because now the fear was all out of proportion.

At her next stop, Bryan Tuckerman swore up and down he hadn't signed any Densmore drawing during his internship at Barrett and Ziko. He gave them a handwriting sample and slogged through the mud of the construction site back to work.

As Gabrielle turned back to her car, she noticed Christian's shoulders were slumped again. "Something bothering you about Bryan?"

"I remember him. He seemed in awe of me. He hung on every word I spoke. Now he thinks I'm a killer."

"Not now he doesn't."

"I was some kind of hero to him. Now I'm not. Even if he no longer thinks I'm a killer, he doesn't think I'm a hero either."

"I'm sorry."

"Yeah."

The impulse grabbed her and wouldn't let go. She wanted to extend this time with him and lift that heavy weight from his shoulders.

Before she could stop it, the words tumbled out of her mouth. "Would you like to have dinner with me?"

CHAPTER 11

Christian couldn't believe he was having dinner with his enemy. Well, she wasn't his enemy exactly. But just because Gabrielle Healey wasn't trying to put him behind bars anymore, didn't make her his friend, either.

He wished to God she was his friend. He could use one right now on a day when he'd alienated his last one. Even more, he wished she was more than his friend. What he wouldn't give to lie naked in her arms and let the solace of her warm body soothe him.

He'd seen the sympathy in her eyes. At first he'd thought it was pity and he'd hated it. But after she'd told him about her mother and the stroke, he realized she knew what he was feeling. Then her sympathy warmed him and made him ache to be held in her arms.

Boy, was he a slow learner. Hadn't he realized yet the world wasn't what it seemed? Gabrielle wasn't romantically interested in him and this wasn't a date.

But their dinner conversation had touched on many aspects of their lives, almost as if this was a first date and they were getting to know one another. They discussed their plan of attack for the following day, and then the conversation swung back to the personal again. That's when the uncertainty of his future nagged at him.

Gabrielle touched his arm lightly, but it was like an electric current jolted through him as soon as she laid her hand on him. She tried to jerk away, but he grabbed her hand and held on. For the first time in weeks, he didn't feel alone. Warmth flooded him and he felt connected to another human being.

"Let go." Her voice sounded strangled.

"I can't." He needed that connection like he needed his next breath. Even more than that.

96

Gabrielle tugged hard on her hand. Her desperate blue glare crossed his, and a jolt of need ran through him, strong enough to steal his breath. He could easily picture the two of them in bed, their naked bodies seething together toward oneness. He got an immediate hard-on.

"No." She drew out the word.

"Come home with me."

"I don't do flings."

"How do you know what it would come to? Why can't you give it a chance?"

"There's no future in this. You're feeling vulnerable right now, so you're turning to the first handy female."

"That's not true." He'd never felt this electricity before. This need.

"Yes it is. It's called propinquity. We're together in the same place at a time when you need to turn to someone. We've been together all day, so you feel a comfort level with me you didn't feel before. You're confusing need and comfort with something else."

Was that what he was feeling? Doubt crept in, making him loosen his hold. Gabrielle snatched her hand away and tucked it beneath the table. He felt cold and bereft without her touch, and strangely less aware of her. When he'd touched her, his senses had felt heightened—now they felt muffled.

"It's not propinquity." How could he explain what he didn't understand? But he tried. "There's something about you..."

Gabrielle stiffened. Her blue eyes iced over, but before they did, he thought he caught a glimpse of wariness. "You're mistaken. If you're finished, I need to get home."

Shut out. It was something he'd experienced with greater frequency in the past few weeks.

"Gabrielle..."

But she stood, a clear sign she didn't want to talk about... whatever it was he'd felt any more. Christian sighed and stood, too.

He didn't argue when Gabrielle grabbed the check and paid it. She had control issues. Whatever glimpses of hurt he'd caught, she clamped down on them quickly. She hid her wariness under a brusque business exterior. The simple act of touching seemed to disturb her. Everything about her screamed "back off."

Christian wished he could heed the signs.

As she stood at her car door, her back stiff, he wanted to take her in his arms and give her comfort. Scoffing at his foolishness, he strode to his Jeep. Right now, he was inadequate to give solace to anyone, even himself. Gabrielle needed a man as confident as she was, a man like he'd been last month.

So why did he feel she needed him as strongly as he needed her?

CHAPTER 12

The next morning, as Gabrielle waited for Christian to arrive, she grappled with her doubts about spending more time with him. She hadn't had a moment's peace since the restaurant yesterday when he'd grabbed her hand and a vision of them making love had blasted through her mind. It had been so real she'd felt his thrusts inside her. She'd felt a connection and oneness with him she'd never felt with another man.

The vision showed her the sex between them would be explosive. Christian would bring the same intensity to lovemaking that he devoted to drawing. She'd never experienced sex like that. All night erotic dreams had mimicked the vision, stimulating her almost to climax.

She didn't know how she was going to spend the day with him without overheating or giving in to her desire. Already her bra felt too tight and her nipples too sensitive for the satin cups. Her panties were damp from the moisture seeping from her body, readying itself for pleasure. If he even touched her…

Her fear surged anew, as fresh as it had been yesterday. If she changed nothing, the prophetic vision showed she would give herself to him. Because she was psychic, she didn't do casual sex, and with Christian, it couldn't be casual, not when everything about him called to her, including his vulnerability. Every moment in his presence, she felt more drawn to him. She would give him everything, including her soul. She'd be more vulnerable than she'd been with any other man, and that would give him the power to destroy her.

When the black Jeep pulled into her drive at seven-thirty, she hurried out to the car. She'd never been a coward and she wasn't about to start now. She had to find the forger quickly to prevent the vision of her and Christian from coming true.

She opened the car door. "Good morning."

"Morning."

He watched her like a cat watches a mouse as she settled into the seat. His eyes were a molten blue, his gaze sizzling enough to scorch. She knew why she was hot and bothered this early in the morning, but why was he? She refused to ask him.

The aroma of fresh coffee rose from his metal travel cup. Under that was the scent of soap and a citrusy aftershave. His face held the sheen of a close shave—touchable.

She wrenched her eyes away, her heart pounding in her chest. Her gaze caught on his long fingers wrapped around the steering wheel. She'd dreamed of them on her body, doing intimate things, most of the night.

Then she noticed the car wasn't moving. "Shall we go?" The less time she had to spend trapped with him in a car, the better…for both their sakes.

Almost against her will, she studied him as he drove. Christian wore a navy blue polo shirt and blue jeans. The dark colors looked good with his black hair, giving him a strikingly handsome appearance. At the moment, that haunting vulnerability was gone, as he handled the Jeep with easy familiarity.

She shook off the fascination he held for her and sought something to say to break the stilted silence. "Your intern, Amir Rahmin, called me last night."

Christian glanced at her, then looked back at the road. "What did he say? I assume he's not the one—otherwise you would have called me and cancelled today's trip."

"You're right. He says he didn't touch the drawing. He's faxing his handwriting sample to Kernfelter later this morning." He'd also told her Christian's partner had built the Densmore because Christian had been designing other contracts. He hadn't personally overseen the construction. That's why she hadn't been able to picture Christian on the third floor.

"I need to call Bryce and tell him," Christian said.

"Who's he?"

"Bryce Gannon, my lawyer."

At the name, she jerked. He was the young man Paul and Roger had pulled from the wooden cage in the water.

"Is he a friend of your brother's?"

Christian shot her a piercing look. "Yeah. His frat brother. Paul's close with several of them."

She wondered if Sean from the vision was one of them, but there was no way to ask that question without revealing what she was.

"You're lucky your brother looks out for you."

Christian grimaced. "I thought so, too."

She heard the "but" he didn't voice. Was it a remnant from yesterday? "Did you talk to your brother last night?"

"No. I tried calling, but he didn't answer. I think he's avoiding me."

"Maybe he just needs a few days to cool off."

Christian's silence spoke volumes, some of it accusatory.

She felt like apologizing, but checked that impulse. He'd agreed they had to question his brother and insisted on coming with her. She'd hated being the one to disillusion him.

The visit to Piggott Concrete eliminated them as a suspect.

The stop after that was Republic Steel, a huge, aging facility. Clearly it hadn't seen an infusion of capital lately. Smokestacks stabbed the sky, belching smoke into the atmosphere.

As Gabrielle climbed out of the Jeep, Christian reached into the back seat and drew out a black golf umbrella. At her inquiring look, he shrugged.

"It's going to rain again soon and it's a hundred yards to the front door. I'm tired of getting soaked. My umbrella's big enough for two." He said it with a straight face.

Gabrielle fought the butterflies fluttering in her stomach. He didn't mean anything intimate by his remark. But she thought about sharing an umbrella, how close they'd have to be. He'd hold it with one hand while he clasped her around the waist with the other to keep her pressed close.

Whoa, girl. He's not for you.

Walking side by side with Christian made her realize he was only four or five inches taller than her five foot seven. They'd fit perfectly together, in every way. Despite the cloud cover, her body felt overheated. She had to get her hormones under control. Obviously, she'd been too long without a man.

They approached the reception desk where a middle-aged brunette watched them with a carefully pleasant face.

Gabrielle introduced herself and told the woman why she was there. "I need to speak with whichever account representative worked on the Densmore project."

"That may take a little while to figure out. You're welcome to wait over there." The receptionist waved to a seating area where half a dozen men and women sat.

Gabrielle and Christian found two seats together. A man with a blueprint carrier stared at Christian with cold hazel eyes.

"Ziko," the man finally said. "What are you doing here?" His dark brown hair was cut short, his jaw squared, his body long and trim.

"Business. And you, Bob?"

The people around them stared. Gabrielle had noticed several of them showed recognition at Christian's name.

"Business. I didn't realize you were working." Bob didn't mention that Christian had been in jail. "I'm curious about your company and about what's going to happen to it when you're no longer...free."

"That's not going to happen."

Bob gave a humorless laugh. "You're delusional if you think that."

Gabrielle could tell Christian was angry by the muscle ticking in his jaw. But Bob's attitude jangled her memory about who would benefit from a frame.

"What company do you represent?" she asked before Christian could escalate the tension with a reply.

"He's Bob Cranston with Hoepflmeier, Dortmouth and Cranston Architects," Christian said.

"Ah. That explains it then. A competitive rival. Professional jealousy." She crossed the space to Cranston and held out her hand. She needed to read him right here and now.

Cranston stood, towering over her. Automatically he gave her his hand, but he frowned as he did it.

The vision was not what Gabrielle expected.

An older man tossed some papers on the desk in front of Bob Cranston. "I assume you heard the Golden Boy's building collapsed."

"Yeah, who hasn't?"

"Those are the contracts we lost to Barrett and Ziko. None of them are started yet. I want you to contact each of them and see if they want to reconsider our bid."

"We don't even know what caused the collapse."

"Doesn't matter. Some people will get nervous, and we want to be there when they do. Give them an alternative and they'll trade allegiances."

Cranston looked from the papers to the older man. "That's cold, Ted."

"That's good business. A partner has to make the most of every opportunity. Make those calls, Bob."

Gabrielle released Bob's hand. So he was innocent of the frame. It wasn't as clear about his partner's involvement, so she'd better give his name to Christian's lawyer and investigate him. This Ted person could have colluded with someone in Christian's firm, like Brittany, to bring Barrett and Ziko down. A desire to increase market share was a powerful motive.

Gabrielle leaned in toward him to speak quietly. Cranston leaned forward as well.

"Michigan Casualty wondered who would benefit from the Densmore's collapse. I should have thought of your company sooner. Do you have time now for some questions?"

Cranston jerked back as though she'd slapped him. "What?"

"Is now a convenient time? How long do you have before your appointment?"

"You're crazy," he tried to keep his voice low. "My company didn't have anything to do with that. It was him." He nodded toward Christian.

"I'd be interested in knowing how much business that originally belonged to Barrett and Ziko now belongs to your firm. It'll be easy enough to find out."

He paled. "Jesus, you're serious."

"Of course. That's my job."

"Mr. Cranston?" the receptionist called.

Cranston turned his head toward the receptionist like he was being thrown a life preserver and then back to Gabrielle again. "I've got a meeting." He bent, snatched up his blueprint carrier and beat a hasty retreat to the front of the lobby.

Gabrielle returned to Christian. As she sat back down, she noted the curious eyes on her.

"What'd you say to him?" Christian asked in a low voice. "He turned white."

"Tell your lawyer to add his firm's name to people who would benefit from framing you."

Christian's eyes widened. "You can't think Cranston would do something like that to get business?"

"Are you going to start arguing with me over suspects again? I thought we got past that yesterday."

He scowled like a sulky boy. "I can't believe it of Bob."

"Maybe not Bob, but he's got partners. Either way, they're

viable suspects. Your lawyer wants to find directions to point the investigation. Bob's firm profited—or will profit—from your business problems. That's called motive. I'll have to pay them a visit this afternoon."

"You've got balls."

Gabrielle tried to decide if he'd given her a compliment or a putdown. "I'm just doing my job."

She had to use those balls to get the home address and phone number of Jerry Flanders, the Republic sales rep who'd handled the Densmore order, when they found out he'd been laid off in the downsizing a few months earlier. Only this time Christian didn't seem too happy about it.

The expected rain had begun while they were inside. Christian opened his large black umbrella and wrapped an arm around her waist to hold her close.

This vision was of them kissing, hungrily devouring each other's mouths. When Christian turned her to face him, she thought it was the vision. But his warm lips on hers were real. He was just as hungry as the man in the vision, and so was she. She'd forgotten how wonderful the first throes of dating could be, when hope was a shining beacon bathing everything with color and light. When a man's touch made her breathless, expectant, eager. When a kiss meant everything.

Christian's tongue prodded her lips for entry. When she opened her mouth and let him in, the glide of his tongue on hers was pure magic. She moaned into his mouth.

Christian gathered her in close to his hard body. In her mind and in real life she was pressed to him, a dual stimulation. She was unable to separate the two, until he entered her in the vision and their striving for oneness began. In real time, he pressed his burgeoning erection to her belly. She wanted what he offered, the real man and the dream, wanted the solace of warm arms, wanted not to be alone, wanted the dream of love everlasting…even if it was a lie.

Someone bumped them. "Excuse me."

Gabrielle became aware of the rain plunking on the taut umbrella, of thunder in the distance, of their proximity to the front door of Republic, of the carnal scene still playing out to its inevitable conclusion in her mind. Heat washed her cheeks, for what they'd been doing in front of possible witnesses, and because of the other scene he couldn't possibly be aware of.

There was only so far she could pull away from him and remain dry, but she needed to be free of his touch. "Let go of me."

"No. I don't know what it is when I touch you, but I can't let you go."

He tugged her toward the parking lot and she went willingly. In her head, she and Christian achieved orgasm and he collapsed onto her, searching for her lips. Somehow she knew he would make love to her again, and she wanted to be away from Christian's touch before then.

Rain splashed around them as they ran to the car. Lightning flashed and thunder crashed overhead. When Christian tried to push her in the back door, she balked.

"What are you doing?"

"I want to make love to you. Now."

"No." She yanked away from him.

He tried to grab her back, but she stepped from underneath the umbrella. Immediately the rain began to soak through her clothes.

"You're getting wet. Climb in the car and I'll warm you like I've been dreaming of doing."

He couldn't be referring to the vision. "We don't have that kind of relationship."

"The hell we don't. I made love to you all night long."

Breath left her. She'd dreamed of making love to him last night, but it couldn't be the same dream. They just shared lust and an undeniable attraction to each other, that's all. It was natural they'd both have x-rated dreams.

"Just a few minutes ago you were criticizing me. Now you want to have sex. I don't think so." She shook her head to emphasize her rejection.

"A minute ago you were plastered to me and your hips were moving against mine. We wanted the same thing. I still do. No one's going to see us in this downpour."

Gabrielle should have been cold, being almost wet to the skin, but his words heated her blood to boiling. Her nipples pebbled and she was sure he could see them through her wet shirt. There was an aching emptiness between her legs she knew he could fill and fill well. But having sex with him in a car in the parking lot of Republic Steel was out of the question.

She stalked around the car and got in on the passenger side. For a moment, Christian continued to stand in the rain. Then he shoved his umbrella between the back seats, and climbed in. His face was dark with temper and something else, the skin taut across his cheekbones.

"I need you," he said between gritted teeth.

And she needed him. "I know you do. I also know why."

He turned to face her. His pupils were still enlarged with arousal. "It's you I want, not just any woman. Did you refuse because I haven't been proved innocent yet?"

She shook her head. "No." She fought the urge to touch him. Maybe if she admitted part of the truth to him. "Christian, I have bad luck with men. I've been hurt more than once. I can't have meaningless sex, and I'm afraid of anything more."

"I won't hurt you, Gabrielle. This hunger I have for you isn't something that's going to be appeased in a few days. Every time I touch you I go mad with the desire to make love with you. Hell, I don't even have to touch you to want you."

"You may not mean to hurt me, but you will. It's not a lifetime commitment you're looking for."

"We have to begin somewhere, but you won't even give me a chance."

"I'm sorry." There were so many reasons why they shouldn't make love. Loneliness shouldn't be the reason they did.

As Christian retraced their path back to the road, Gabrielle regretted not being able to lie in his arms. She still felt the imprint of his naked chest on her breasts, of his belly against hers, of his weight on her. She wanted all that, with the desperation of a woman who hadn't had sex in nearly two years.

DesignCorp was located in a new glass building on a block that looked like the old was slowly being replaced by the new.

Christian retrieved his umbrella and walked around to her side of the car. Although she didn't want him to touch her, she didn't want to get any wetter. Already she was going to look like a drowned rat when she presented herself.

She was ready this time when Christian wrapped his arm around her, or so she thought. The feel of his penis sliding wetly in and out of her was incredibly real. The intimate stretching was arousing. The rub of his chest across her nipples brought them to points. Christian groaned. Wait, that sound came from the man next to her.

She turned to look at him. His eyes were nearly black with arousal. His skin was the dusky color of a man making love.

"God, I've got to have you. That feels so real."

She jerked. He was seeing it, too. But that was impossible. She was panting hard, and not from what they were doing in the vision. Never had a man shared that part of her mind. Why now? Why this man?

When they entered the lobby, the cold air conditioning brushed across her wet skin and clothes. Her nipples, already taut, tightened painfully into nubs and she shivered.

Christian stepped away from her to shake out the umbrella and she breathed a sigh of relief to be released from his arousing nearness.

DesignCorp was the opposite of Republic Steel. The décor

bespoke newness and a recent infusion of capital. The lobby gleamed with a faux marble floor.

The receptionist was young, with straight blonde hair, the upper half pulled back in a claw clip. "May I help you?"

Gabrielle went through the now-familiar spiel.

But the young woman frowned. "I'm sorry, Ms. Healey, but no one here is to speak with you or Mr. Ziko."

Christian said, "But we need to talk to whoever did the testing for the Densmore Building."

"I'm sorry, but I have my orders from the president of the company. You'll have to leave."

"I don't understand," Gabrielle protested. "Why aren't you allowed to speak to us?"

"We received a subpoena half an hour ago. That's when the president of DesignCorp said we weren't to talk to anyone, especially Mr. Ziko."

"But you've got evidence pertinent to Mr. Ziko's case and important to my investigation. We have to see it," Gabrielle said.

"We'll provide our information to the court. Please, I'm not allowed to speak with you."

Christian took hold of Gabrielle's arm and moved her out of hearing range of the reception desk. He pulled out his cell phone and dialed a number.

"It's Kit," he said into the receiver.

Gabrielle could hear the agitated male voice on the other end, but not the words.

"I'm your friend," Christian said. "What do you mean you can't talk to me?"

The voice dropped too low for Gabrielle to hear.

"No, man, I don't want to jeopardize your job, but I don't want to go to jail, either. I need to see the test results for the Densmore."

Christian listened intently, his face darkening. "No, I understand. It's nothing personal." His voice sounded bitter.

Whatever his friend said next relaxed his face and his posture. "No, I believe you. Thanks for telling me. I'll still see you next weekend?"

The reply made Christian's lips curl at the corner, almost a smile. "Yeah, me too. See you."

He ended the call and tucked his phone away.

"So it's true?" Gabrielle asked.

"Yeah. The president of DesignCorp placed a gag order on the employees. Whoever talks gets canned, no matter what."

"Damn. I wanted to see the evidence. Now we'll have to wait until they respond to the subpoena."

"We'll get nowhere here." Christian urged her toward the glass doors. "Where else do we need to go?"

"I'm going to visit your rival Cranston's firm. Do you know where it is?"

Christian smirked. "Warren, a few miles from Kernfelter's office."

"You can drop me at Cranston's and take the samples to Kernfelter."

"Okay. That works for me."

They used the umbrella once they were outside in the rain. This time the vision was worse because Christian was sucking her breasts. She bit back a groan in real life, although her vision self experienced no such restraint.

"Back seat, please," Christian pleaded.

She wanted it as much as he did, but she had to be strong. "Get in and drive, Christian."

He growled with frustration, but did as she asked. "I've never had such clear thoughts of being with a woman."

Gabrielle sucked in her breath. Visions were like that. "You've got a vivid imagination, Christian."

He gave her a long look, then started the car.

Traffic was moving fast as they approached the Chrysler

Freeway, with cars darting to the lanes drivers wanted to be in. In the steadily falling rain, red taillights flashed on and off ahead of them.

Christian was trying to merge into the left lane for the Chrysler when a large dark SUV cut them off. There was nowhere to go so Christian slammed on the brakes. The Jeep slid toward the concrete divider. Another vehicle hit them in the rear, driving the Jeep hard into the concrete.

The collision was jarring. It threw Gabrielle forward against her seatbelt and then to the left. Horns blared around them. Brakes screamed. She braced herself for another impact, but luck must have been with them, because cars continued to pass them, their red brake lights indicating they were at least slowing down, if not stopping.

"Can we move?" Gabrielle asked.

When Christian said nothing, she looked at him harder. His head leaned against the driver's window and he was completely still.

"Christian?" She reached over and touched him. For the first time in her life, she read nothing. It was like white noise in her head. She knew he must be unconscious.

She tugged on his arm. Like a rag doll, his head rolled toward her. Blood seeped down the left side of his face from a cut above his brow.

CHAPTER 13

Christian left the North Detroit General Hospital ER with a concussion, a bottle of pain pills, a bad case of nausea, and an even worse case of mortification. He hated looking pathetic in front of Gabrielle. This was a woman he wanted to take to bed and make scream with pleasure. He didn't want her feeling pity or disgust while he was incapacitated.

The ER doctor had told Christian someone had to wake him every hour, so he'd begged Gabrielle to stay with him. Now she drove the rental car to his condo in Bloomfield Hills. He fought down nausea, hoping to avoid further humiliation. An interminable twenty minutes later they pulled into his driveway. None too soon, as far as he was concerned.

The car was immediately mobbed by reporters.

"Mr. Ziko, what do you feel your chances are for a dismissal?" one shouted.

"Who do you feel is guilty, if not you?" another asked.

"Mr. Ziko, what happened to your head?"

Had he known reporters would be here, he would have let Gabrielle take the samples to Kernfelter and nausea be damned.

She came around the side of the rental car, and to his dismay, helped him out. He hoped he wouldn't have sexual daydreams about her in front of the press when she took hold of his arm. What he got, besides the sensual jolt of skin on skin, was a feeling of coming home. His skin buzzed with electricity where they touched.

Cameras flashed. The bright light of a camcorder caught his helplessness on film. Shit.

"Are you trying for the sympathy vote?" one caustic voice called.

"Clear a path," Gabrielle said.

"Who's she?" a reporter asked.

Damn. Any hope of keeping Gabrielle's anonymity went out the window. At least she'd removed her nametag. But enterprising reporters would dig until they found out who she was.

"No comment," he said.

Someone stuck a microphone in his face. "Mr. Ziko, how do you feel about the new subpoenas handed down today?"

"I said, no comment."

"Murderer!" a male voice yelled from the back of the crowd.

Gabrielle stopped, making Christian grab her as he lurched. Half the reporters thrust microphones in his face, the other half rushed to provide an equal forum for a young man in his early twenties. His brown hair was buzz cut, his T-shirt displayed muscular arms and chest, and his face was red with anger...and hatred.

"Murderer," the young man repeated with fervor. "You killed my sister Gina. You need to pay for what you did, Ziko."

What could Christian say to this young man? He knew how it felt to lose someone you loved. But he wasn't guilty.

"It wasn't my fault."

The young man stalked toward Christian in a threatening manner. No one tried to stop him. "She was my only family. You killed her, the same as if you'd shot her."

"Christian," Gabrielle said.

"What's your name?" Christian asked.

The young man stopped and drew himself up straighter. "Wes. Wes Masterson. You'd better remember it because I'm going to make sure you pay for what you did. Your high-priced lawyer won't help you slip away from the charges. I know you're guilty, and so does everyone here." His arm waved over the army of reporters.

Gabrielle tugged on Christian's arm, forcing him toward the house.

Christian had almost reached his front door when Masterson got in his face. "You deserve to go to jail. You deserve worse than jail. My sister's dead while you're still walking around."

"We're trying to find who killed your sister," Christian said.

"You killed my sister. You're trying to make people doubt the truth." He poked Christian in the chest.

Christian understood the young man's rage, his desire to make somebody hurt the way he was hurting. Christian had felt that way when his parents died. So he let Wes vent. If Christian got angry, it would only escalate the confrontation.

"I know you're hurting—"

"Don't pretend you know how I feel or that you sympathize with me."

Gabrielle stepped between them. "You've had your say, now you'd better leave."

"What are you, this coward's mouthpiece? Are you his damn lawyer?"

Gabrielle lowered her voice. "I'm a citizen witnessing someone intent on committing a crime. Unless you want to see some jail time, I suggest you leave."

Masterson's hands clenched into fists. "You haven't heard the last of me." He stalked off across the lawn.

"Get me inside." Christian was near the end of his strength, both physically and emotionally.

The reporters looked ready to converge when Gabrielle opened the door and pulled him inside. As soon as she closed the door, Christian slid down the wall in a slump.

CHAPTER 14

Gabrielle couldn't have caught Christian if she'd tried. She leaped to his side as his butt hit the floor.

"Christian."

His hand came up to feebly wave her off. "I'm all right. Just leave me be." He sank his head into his hands.

"You didn't kill his sister," she said.

"I know that. You know that. But he doesn't believe me when I tell him the truth. To the world, I'm still a murderer."

"Not to your lawyer. Not to Kernfelter."

He looked at her with anguish in his eyes. "I want the people that matter to know the truth." He waved toward the door. "Him, and the other relatives. I know how helpless and lost Masterson feels. I've been there. It hurts just to look at him and know I can't help him. But it hurts even more knowing he thinks I'm to blame."

"He won't have long to wait until we learn the truth."

"He needs to know the truth now. I need people to know the truth now." His voice dropped to a whisper. "I've never been hated before. I don't like it."

There was the vulnerable man again, the very human, fragile being. Gabrielle felt compelled to touch him, to ease his pain.

But how did she help him? Now when Christian needed some surety to hold onto, Gabrielle's 'gift' was useless. It couldn't be programmed to look at the future, much less a specific timeframe in the future.

She touched him anyway, because for most people, human contact was comforting. To her, it meant visions.

This one was of Christian as a teenager. His face was ravaged by grief as he stood before a double grave. Sod had not yet been laid over the dirt, nor had the headstones been set in place.

115

The young Christian's fists clenched. "Why?" he demanded of the sky. "Why did you take them? I need them."

The vision blurred out, as though there was too much emotion in the memory. Christian had shared their sexual daydreams. Had he relived this one as well and couldn't face that memory anymore? Had he belatedly raised his natural shields?

"Don't touch me." Christian's voice was hoarse.

"Let me help you to your bed so you can lie down."

"I can lie down right here."

Gabrielle huffed a breath. "Christian, you're being stubborn. Your bed is much more comfortable."

"Why should I be comfortable when innocent people are lying in graves? Someone took something I created and made a deathtrap out of it. Even when I'm cleared of the charges, people will still associate my name with the Densmore disaster. How will I handle that?"

"You just go on."

"Is that what you're doing? Going on after someone hurt you?"

Gabrielle released his arm. She couldn't let him see he was on target. Her pain was private, her insecurities and doubts better off hidden from the world.

"C'mon, I'm moving you to your bedroom."

Gabrielle braced her feet and tugged Christian up. She ignored the resultant vision as best she could. She had enough to deal with right now.

When he was on his feet, groaning and holding his head in pain, she guided him slowly across the living room to the wide doorway she assumed was the master bedroom. His condo was fairly new, the walls a neutral cream, the dark molding a pleasing contrast. His furniture, chocolate brown leather, invited her to sink into its supple depths. The effect was very masculine.

His bedroom was just as masculine, with big walnut pieces. The queen-sized bed was her fantasy come true, with four tall posts and a plush burgundy comforter.

Underneath, the sheets were burgundy and cream striped. She wondered if some old girlfriend had helped him pick out the bedding. She fought down jealousy, having no reason to be envious of any woman in Christian's life.

She helped Christian lie down in the bed and with a groan, he stretched out. His left hand clutched his forehead near the white bandage.

"Do you want your medication?" she asked.

"Not yet. My stomach has to settle first. Then I have to call my doctor. I need my address book on the desk in the kitchen."

As she left the room, Gabrielle attributed his curt tone to the pain in his head. She located the address book on the small built-in desk, but when she lifted it, a small piece of paper fluttered out. The name Sean Bergman screamed at her from it. When she picked it up, she got a picture of the man from the earlier vision—the one that included Christian's brother, his partner and his lawyer—only this time he was older, with brown hair graying on the sides. What was he to Christian?

Gabrielle carried the address book back to the bedroom. Christian's left hand massaged his temple, probably trying to ease his headache. His eyes were closed.

"I found the book," Gabrielle said.

Christian's lids flew open, uncovering blue eyes darkened with pain. She stepped close to him and handed him the small book.

"This fell out." She handed him the piece of paper.

His fingers brushed hers as he took it, resulting in a vision.

The older Sean wrote quickly on a sheet of paper, tore it off and handed it to Christian. "Here, take my number. Call me day or night, no matter what. I'm here for you."

"I won't need you," Christian said.

"I'll feel better knowing you have my number."

Christian pulled away from her and the vision was lost. "Thanks." His voice was gruff. "Would you mind giving me a little privacy for this call?"

She wanted very much to hear what he had to say to his doctor, but obviously Christian didn't want her to hear. Did he have a medical condition that wasn't public knowledge?

Gabrielle scoffed at herself. Maybe Christian was intensely private about his health…like she was about her clairvoyance.

Down a short hall to the right was Christian's office. Every surface was piled with papers and blueprints and notes, reminding her of Roger Barrett's office yesterday. Christian had a modern, well-equipped office in Troy, yet it looked like he worked here as well. He loved his job so much, he couldn't turn it off when he got home. It was sad, in a way. Of course, who was she to judge?

The dining room held an older maple table and six chairs. Suddenly she realized what she was seeing. She stroked her finger across a chair back and confirmed the set had belonged to Christian's parents. She wondered if his bedroom furniture was also his inheritance.

She thought about how tightly he held onto his past. She couldn't imagine having lost her mother during her teen years, and surely Christian had a more normal relationship with his parents than she had with her mother. He must have been devastated to lose them.

The refrigerator shelves were mostly bare, except for some yogurt, which a quick check proved to be expired. Christian had said he'd been away and her palm on the door confirmed it. But his office looked like he'd been here working. Which was true?

She heard a muffled sound, but couldn't place it. She froze, cocking her head. In a moment, it came again. Smiling to herself because it was Christian calling for her from behind the closed bedroom door, she went to him.

He lay back against his pillow, his face white and drawn, tracking her movements with his eyes. "I need your assistance."

Gabrielle came to the edge of the bed, but didn't touch him. "What do you need?"

His blue eyes darkened further. "What I need, you won't give me."

In the pause that followed, she couldn't reply. The need in his eyes was tinged with something like the fact that his dining room set was how he clung to his parents. She didn't want him clinging to her during these desperate hours just because he had no one else. Because eventually his desperation would ease.

Gabrielle swallowed and ignored Christian's words.

In a moment, he sighed and spoke again, this time in a flat tone. "I can have half a pain pill. Would you cut several in half for me?"

"Sure. Anything else?"

"My cell phone. I need to call my brother before he hears what happened from someone else."

"You should probably call your lawyer, too."

"Right."

She turned to retrieve his cell phone from her purse, but his voice recalled her attention.

"Gabrielle?"

"Yes?"

"I'm sorry the news cameras caught you with me. I know you wanted to be discreet."

Damn. She hadn't thought of that. Now she had something else to worry about.

CHAPTER 15

Christian's phone call to his brother raised his blood pressure enough to double the throbbing in his head.

"Are you sure someone cut you off?" Paul asked, after hearing about the accident and Christian's injury.

"Yes, I'm sure. Cars were swerving in and out of traffic, driving crazy in the rain."

"Maybe it wasn't an accident."

His brother's tone puzzled Christian. "What do you mean?"

Paul's sigh gusted over the phone. "Christian, are you taking your meds?"

Gritting his teeth sent shards of pain into his head. "You think I ran into the divider on purpose?" It was difficult keeping his voice down so Gabrielle wouldn't hear through the open door. "I told you I'm not suicidal."

"It just seems too coincidental that out of the million people in Detroit, you'd be involved in an accident."

"I wasn't the only one. We saw quite a few fender benders. It was just a freak thing that I hit my head."

"Kit, you're not acting like yourself. First you make accusations against me, now this. Maybe I should have a talk with Sean."

Christian's blood pressure skyrocketed until he thought he might have a stroke. "There's nothing wrong with me, and I've already spoken to Sean."

"What'd he say?"

"That's none of your business. He's my doctor, so what's between us is private."

"I'll call him and talk to him."

Suddenly Christian was tired of being treated like a child. He'd be damned if their fraternity connection allowed Sean to spill his

120

latest consultation to his brother. Or allowed Paul to dictate his treatment plan.

"Paul, I'm hanging up now and calling Sean. I'm going to tell him if he says one word to you about me, I'll file a suit against him under HIPAA." He hung up before he could allow his brother's pleading to sway him.

Guilt washed over him, hot and nauseating. Paul had always taken care of him, always watched out for him. He'd known what Christian needed both times he'd fallen into serious depressions. He should listen to his brother.

No. He was thirty-two years old. He was back on his medication and no longer depressed. He was taking control of his life. He dialed Sean.

In less than two minutes, he'd laid down the law to Sean, revoking Paul's HIPAA privileges. No matter what Sean owed to Paul, Christian was his patient. Sean was reluctant at first, which solidified Christian's resolve to break from him.

As soon as he hung up, his cell rang. Wary, Christian looked at the number before answering. Shit. The other fraternity brother. His lawyer.

"Hello, Bryce."

"What's going on? Paul just called me, ranting that you'd gone crazy and had an accident. He says we need to get you back in Crittenden right away."

Damn those frat brothers. "Who do you work for, Bryce?" He channeled all his anger into his voice, making it as sharp as broken glass.

There was a telling pause. "So we're back to that again."

"Yes. Either you believe in me, or I find another lawyer."

"Tell me what happened." Bryce's voice was as neutral as it had been in his office yesterday.

Anger still burned in Christian's veins. His temple throbbed with the force of his blood pressure. But he gave Bryce the details of the accident and added everything he and Gabrielle had learned along the way.

"So there are several suspects. I'll file the request for a subpoena for Jeremy Barrett's handwriting. The sooner Kernfelter analyzes the other samples, the sooner we'll have evidence to present in your defense."

"Any word on the request to dismiss?"

"Nothing yet. I'll call you as soon as I hear anything."

"Bryce, I need you not to report to Paul. I'm your client. If I want Paul to know something, I'll tell him."

Another long pause, much like the one from Sean. "My relationship with your brother is long-standing."

Christian waited. Either Bryce was on his side…or he wasn't. Still, Christian was uneasy having to remind the frat brothers that he was their client. Why had it become him versus Paul?

"All right," Bryce said. "I'll call when I have any updates."

Christian tossed the phone onto the bed beside him. He felt sick, and not just from the concussion. He'd never felt more alone than he did at this moment. Although he'd gotten both Sean and Bryce's agreement, he didn't trust either man. At this moment, he wasn't even sure he trusted his brother.

He had made one mistake, and suddenly in Paul's eyes he was that seventeen-year-old boy who couldn't take care of himself. That doubt hurt, cutting deep. Now Paul didn't trust him, and neither did Paul's friends. They wondered if he was a bomb about to explode. He was glad they couldn't see him now, lying helpless in bed, unable to marshal his own defense against the criminal charges. He was pathetic.

A sound drew his gaze to the doorway where Gabrielle stood, her blue eyes concerned but her stance wary.

"I'm sorry. I couldn't help overhearing some of your conversation."

He was tempted to look away, but he was through hiding from difficult things in life. "I need a different lawyer, but I really shouldn't change right now."

"Because he's your brother's friend?"

"Yeah." He should have known she'd get right to the point. Her intelligence was one of the things he liked about her. "They don't see me for who I really am, but as their friend's little brother who needs to be taken care of. Do you understand?"

Her blue eyes darkened with some deep emotion. "Yes, I understand."

*

Gabrielle left Christian to sleep, or whatever else he planned to do and escaped to the living room, away from the darkness that had taken over his spirit. She wanted to give him comfort and ease his burdens. But that way lay hurt, for if she gave him her strength, she knew she'd also give her heart. She yearned to be yin to his yang. Each time they touched, she felt the possibility of completeness, to interlock together as one. But she was afraid, and the fear kept her from reaching out.

When her cell phone rang, she almost welcomed the interruption of her painful thoughts. But when caller ID showed her boss's number, she didn't want to answer.

"Hi, Cal."

"Gabrielle, what the hell are you doing?"

She tried playing dumb. "What do you mean?"

"You know damn well. I saw you on the news with Ziko. I specifically told you to stay away from him. He's guilty. You need to close your case file and move on to the next case."

"Cal, I'm investigating some new evidence..."

"Not if it lets Ziko off the hook. Michigan Casualty needs not to pay on this claim. Do you understand me?"

"Yes. But Cal, this evidence benefits Michigan Casualty."

There was a pause, and then he demanded. "What is it?"

If she told him the truth and he decided it wasn't worth the risk, he could shut her down. But she told him everything.

"It sounds like a police investigation to me," he said.

"I normally run a concurrent investigation, you know that. I want to tell Michigan Casualty's clients exactly who owes them money, but whether that's Barrett and Ziko or a jealous competitor, I don't know at this time. We owe our clients the truth, Cal."

"Yes, and if there are two culprits, that's even better. Fine, you have forty-eight hours."

"But that's not enough time." Christian wouldn't be mobile for the first twenty-four, but she wouldn't tell Cal that.

"If you need more time than that, then you're not the right person for my job."

What could she respond to that? Nothing. "I'll do my best."

"I know you will." He disconnected the call without saying good-bye.

Gabrielle wanted to scream her frustration. Now she had to make a determination of guilt from among numerous suspects, do it in forty-eight hours, to Cal's satisfaction, and half that time she'd be stuck at Christian's house watching over the invalid. And he didn't even have food or diet soda in the house.

*

When Gabrielle prodded Christian partially awake during the night, he pulled her down onto his bare chest. As he fumbled with her PJs, trying to bare her, she pushed at his chest to get him to release her. She couldn't let the inevitable happen.

"Stay with me. Please." His words were slightly slurred from the pain meds, his pupils dilated, but need dripped from every syllable.

Gabrielle had to swallow her own need before she could reply. "That's not a good idea, Christian."

"The bed's big enough. I need you."

She sighed. She couldn't fight both of them. "All right."

Later, she didn't know who started it, her or him, but it began with a touch. Just one touch. She thought she was having another hot, erotic dream about him. In it, he lifted her short PJ top, or maybe she did. He pulled her down until her breasts touched his bare chest. The electric contact made her suck in her breath. So did he. Then she knew this wasn't a dream. In her head, the vision of her and Christian making love continued, but in reality, it was just beginning. She rubbed her breasts up and down his chest, until her nipples stood out with excitement.

Christian gripped her butt and pulled her fully onto him. Then he yanked her PJ shorts down to mid-thigh. Next, he pulled down his own shorts.

"Christian…" Her protest was weak. The warmth of his genitals against hers felt so good. The vee of her thighs rubbed up and down on his hardened cock, making him groan against her lips, making her wet between her legs.

"I like feeling you against me," he said.

He kissed her. It was a hungry kiss, on both their parts. As she continued to rub herself against him, he shifted, or she did, and his cock slid between her legs. They were flesh to flesh from chest to mid-thigh. Her sigh of relief echoed his. He was where he belonged. They fit together like two puzzle pieces. Well, almost. He wrapped his arms tightly around her back.

Gabrielle purred her pleasure. They rocked together, not just his cock against her cleft but their entire bodies. She'd never felt so complete, so in tune with the man in his arms. She felt electrified.

Gabrielle pressed her nose into the hollow of his throat and kissed his neck. He nuzzled her temple, his breath warm against her face.

"Am I inside you?" he asked, nuzzling her ear.

"No." He was sharing her vision again. She fought down her feelings of unease and turned to kiss his lips.

The echo of the vision continued, arousing her doubly. The real

Christian moved his body urgently against hers, while his dream body moved strongly inside her.

And then one of them shifted again, and suddenly he pushed his fullness inside her body. Gabrielle stiffened, groaning, as she stretched to accommodate him. The sense of coming home was so strong, she knew she would not deny either of them this joining.

"Wait, Christian. We need a condom."

"I'm clean. Are you?"

"Yes, but I'm not on the pill."

"Nightstand drawer." Their vision selves were thrusting faster. Christian thrust into Gabrielle. "Hurry."

As she reached for the nightstand, he moved with her. He thrust upwards and deep as she leaned forward to grab a condom from the drawer. She groaned, her outstretched hand frozen in air as excited tingles ran through her loins. Clutching the condom, she sank onto him and they both groaned. She rested her forehead gently against his.

"I'm not sure we should do this." It was getting hard to think while Christian of the vision thrust into her. That couple's desperation to be complete was becoming her own.

"Gabrielle, I need you." His voice dripped need.

Her sigh gusted across his face. "I need you, too."

She lifted off of him. He grabbed for her, but she turned with the condom in her hand. He stroked her breast and the already tight nipple beaded further. He took the nub between his thumb and forefinger and rotated it. Pleasure shot straight to her lower body. Gabrielle moaned.

So did he when she smoothed the condom on him. She cupped his balls, massaging them with her thumbs. The couple in her mind were mating with frantic need.

"Gabrielle."

She shimmied out of her PJs and mounted him. Their groans were a sedate echo to what she heard in her mind. But as soon as they began to move, their rhythm began to try to sync with the other couple's.

Her body moved naturally with his. There was no hesitation, as though they'd been lovers for years. Yet the frantic sensation grew stronger, not weaker. She had to become one with him.

His body fit inside hers perfectly, filling her up with intimate stretching. His gasps and sighs as she sank on him and lifted once again were music to her ears. The heat of their joining burned through her loins, branding her, branding him.

"Christian..."

"My name is Kit."

"Kit. Call me Gaby."

"I like Gabrielle better."

So did she, the way he said it. She sucked in her breath. "Help me go faster."

Christian grabbed her hips and moved her up and down on him. She got wetter the faster his cock slid in and out. Their pace was almost equal to the vision couple.

And then there was only one pace, and vision became reality. Gabrielle was stunned by the beauty of their loving, by the wonder of having Christian inside her. He held the key to something she hadn't known was missing. She sought it in him as he plumbed her depths. The strength of her orgasm caught her by surprise, and she cried out, grinding her body into his as she milked him.

But Christian grabbed her hips and rolled until she was under him. He pounded into her body with a desperate need. She arched her hips to his with a sharp cry as a second orgasm seized her.

And then they were catapulted into the oneness she sought. She grabbed after it, as he grasped her tight and emptied his passion into her. They flew together, one soul.

But the flight was all too brief. They settled to earth in a gasping, panting pile.

"That was more than I ever imagined making love could be." He sounded slightly out of breath.

"Yes." She'd sensed it was possible with him.

"The dream is gone."

She didn't know how to talk to him about the vision he'd experienced. "Christian…"

"Kit."

"Kit, you see it, too?"

"Yeah. You sound surprised."

"I've never shared a vision with anyone before." Why this man?

"We're different. Don't you feel it when we're together?"

"I don't know what I feel." It was too much to take in while aftershocks trembled through her lower body.

He nuzzled her face. "Don't think so much. This is too new to analyze. We have to face the world soon enough. For these moments, can't we make love again and enjoy each other?"

She cupped his face in her hands and turned it until she could see him in the weak light from the living room. She thought she saw a reflection of what she was feeling, of everything they'd experienced in the past frantic moments. She wasn't the only one who'd felt the oneness. Already, another vision of them making love began. What was to happen between them was fated.

She nodded. "We'll need another condom."

"We have all we need."

CHAPTER 16

As dawn lightened Christian's bedroom, Gabrielle slipped from his arms, careful not to wake him. She showered, washing off the evidence of his multiple possessions. She needed this time alone to face what she'd done.

She'd slept with Christian Ziko. No, that was too mild a description. They'd mated with ferocious need, they'd ravaged one another with a hunger that wouldn't be slaked. Her tender breasts and aching vagina were testimony to his passion.

The visions had continued as she and Christian made love. She thought they might be the reason they had made love three times. It troubled her that he shared her psychic vision.

Why had she agreed to make love with him? She'd tried not to become close to Christian, tried to hold off from becoming intimate. Now, she felt a connection to him. She'd sensed it was possible, but now she was afraid they'd forged a bond impossible to break. And that frightened her more than anything.

"Gabrielle?"

She jerked, startled. Christian stood outside the glass doors, leaning on the wall.

"I'll be right out."

The shower door slid open. "Don't bother."

She tried to avoid his touch, but it was impossible in the small shower. As soon as he touched her, the vision began again, and she knew she was lost. His cock was hard and full once more. She didn't know how he was able after all they'd done already, and pain medicine and a concussion on top of it. But she didn't fight it as he turned her to face the wall.

His warm flesh pressed against her buttocks, and the slick head of his cock probed between her legs as his strong arms slid around her. He thrust inside her.

Gabrielle was helpless against him, against the visions that predicted each coupling with him. It was meant to be. So she moved with him, feeling the connection soul deep.

*

Christian's headache was a steady but bearable throb, his nausea non-existent that morning. They had a full schedule of investigating ahead of them. Their first stop would be the automotive repair shop in Highland Park, where his Jeep had been towed, to retrieve the handwriting samples.

As they surveyed the reporters from his front window, he realized there was no x-rated scene playing like a movie inside his head. There'd been no vision when he'd woken alone, either. But each time he and Gabrielle touched, erotic images filled his mind.

He remembered what she'd said. "Last night, you asked me if I could see the vision, too. What did you mean?"

Gabrielle released the window curtain, the car keys clutched in her hand so hard the tendons stood out. She looked wary. She swallowed but didn't respond.

Christian got a bad feeling in his gut, and it wasn't from concussion hangover. What did they call people who saw things when they touched people? He couldn't remember the technical term, but he did know something.

"You're psychic?" he asked.

Gabrielle flinched. Color slowly leached from her face, leaving her eyes as pain-filled blue orbs. "Yes. We need to go. Don't say anything to the press."

As soon as she opened the front door, several reporters ran toward them. Gabrielle and Christian walked through the barrage of questions without saying a word. She unlocked the car and slid behind the wheel, her movements stiff, as though she was angry.

She didn't want to admit the truth to him. It hurt, the lack of trust, coming so soon after their soul-shattering intimacy.

Christian climbed into the passenger side, angry because he knew he shouldn't drive today. He was cut off from full independence when he had important work to take care of. And he was dependent on Gabrielle when he'd just learned she kept secrets from him.

He waited until they'd reached the main road before he asked. "Tell me the truth. I deserve to know."

"I'm what's called a touch clairvoyant."

"By touch, do you mean just a little?"

"No. I'm sure you've seen TV shows where the psychic holds something in his or her hand and can tell the police where to find a missing child?"

"Yeah. Is that what you do?"

She shook her head. "No, but I know things about an item when I touch it, like if a fire was arson, and I often see the face of the person who set it."

"That must come in handy in your job." The words sounded bitter. She was a freak. He'd slept with a freak. Then full realization made his breath catch. "What about when you touch people?"

"I can see things about them, too."

He had a sinking feeling in the pit of his stomach. "Is that how you knew my brother had an affair with Brittany?"

"Yes."

He had secrets he had to keep. He couldn't ask outright if she'd learned he was bipolar. "What did you learn about me?"

Gabrielle gave him a sharp look, then her eyes shuttered. "You love your work..."

"That's no secret."

"I saw you draw the Densmore. I saw the look in your eyes, the love that went into the drawing. You were barefoot."

He felt more vulnerable in that moment than he'd felt his entire life. He tried to ask a question, but had to clear his throat and begin again. "Anything else?"

"You stood beside the Mackinaw Bridge and you loved that, too. I think you must have wanted to design bridges, but you felt you had to stay close to Paul."

He felt like he was stripped naked in a crowd.

"You stood in front of your parents' graves soon after they died and wanted to know why they'd left you."

God, she knew everything about him. All those times she touched him, she was prying into his mind, ferreting out things about him.

"Did you do it for Michigan Casualty? Do they send you in to determine a person's guilt by touching him or her?"

When she stopped for a red light, she looked at him. It was a look that could freeze a person alive. "My employer doesn't know what I am. Like your reaction, most people are freaked by someone who can sense things by touch. I rarely tell people, and when I do, inevitably, they show fear and loathing like you are."

Three facts jumped out at him from what she'd said. Her employer didn't know. She didn't tell people. And when she did, people hurt her.

That was the hurt he'd sensed from the very beginning. People hurt her...like he was doing now. People judged her...like he had. Did that mean people rejected her because she was psychic? He guessed they did.

"You can't blame me for being..." he searched for a word that wouldn't insult her, "unnerved."

"Of course not. Why should you be different than the rest of Detroit? By all means, be afraid like the masses."

Her pain echoed in him, stabbed his beating heart and made it ache. Her being a psychic was something she couldn't change, like eye color...or bipolar. She didn't sound happy to be able to pick people's minds like cheap locks. She sounded like she hated it, probably because of how people reacted to her. He didn't want to hurt her further, but he needed to understand.

"The vision I've had of making love to you..."

"It's clairvoyant and it's precognitive, meaning it's a prediction of a possible future. You shouldn't be able to sense it, or share it with me."

"Are you using telepathy on me, is that why I see it?"

"I'm not a telepath, as least I never was before. If you're a psychic, that would explain the shared vision."

"I'm not a psychic." Hell, no.

"Have you ever been tested?"

He'd been tested for everything else when he was seventeen, but never that. "No."

"Then you might be."

"I'm not." He had enough to deal with without being that.

The temperature in the car dropped, and it wasn't from the air conditioning. His vehemence about not being psychic hadn't gone over well with Gabrielle. Damn. The morning after a night of lovemaking like they'd experienced shouldn't go this badly. He knew the most intimate things about her, but he didn't really know her. Had he known she was psychic...

Christian pulled in his breath sharply. Would he have avoided going to bed with her if he'd known? Would he have kept an emotional and physical distance from her? His belly felt cold with his doubts. Apparently what she was did make a difference. He didn't like what he learned about himself at that moment. And what was worse, the future he'd been picturing with Gabrielle seemed to have gone up in smoke. Another disillusionment.

After driving the rest of the way in silence, Gabrielle pulled into Dun-rite Auto Repair and parked.

"That's my Jeep in the bay," he said.

As they approached, he saw the driver's side wheel had been removed and a mechanic was working on the suspension.

The mechanic in the adjoining bay looked up from the car he was working on and pulled a rag out of his back pocket to wipe his hands. "Can I help you folks?"

"That's my Jeep," Christian waved his hand toward it. "I need some papers out of it."

"I need to see some ID."

"Sure." Christian handed over his driver's license.

"Ziko. You're the one under indictment." The man's friendly tone had turned icy.

Christian didn't want to explain to this man, but he wanted his car back in working order. He didn't want any "accident" happening to him as a result of purposely faulty repairs. "Yeah. I'm working on proving my innocence. The papers in my Jeep are evidence."

"That right?" The words dripped doubt.

"Yes. If I'd been able to deliver them yesterday, you might have read about my innocence in this morning's paper. But as you can see," he indicated his bandaged head and the Jeep's wheel, "I couldn't do that."

The man handed Christian's license back. "I don't want it said that Donny Nash stood in the way of a man proving his innocence. Take whatever you need out of the car." He turned to the other bay. "Jeff, move out of the way and let these people get their stuff."

The second mechanic rose from his crouch and went to stand by the other.

Christian took the driver's side of the Jeep and Gabrielle took the passenger's.

After a moment of digging, Gabrielle spoke up from the front seat. "It's not here."

Christian looked up from searching the back seat for the copy of the drawing from City Hall. "It must have shifted when we hit the wall. Look under the seat." He did the same.

"It's not here." Her tone was so flat it was obvious she was covering up some emotion.

"Mine's not either." Christian turned to Donny and Jeff, fighting off panic. "Did you empty my car?"

Donny frowned and scratched his head. "No. We didn't touch the inside except to drive it into the bay."

"The evidence is gone. It's very important. Did anybody else touch the car? Who else works here?" He had to have that evidence.

"Just the owner, Harmon Dunn. He opened this morning, but he left to get parts."

"Did he remove any files or papers?" Christian asked.

"Not that I seen."

"When's he due back?"

"Less than an hour."

"Is there somewhere we can wait for him?"

"There's chairs in his office." Donny pointed off to his right.

By the time Christian and Gabrielle had reached the office, his head had begun to pound from his blood pressure rising. When he looked back, Donny and Jeff were peering into his Jeep.

He turned to Gabrielle. "Do you think somebody took the papers?"

"Don't panic. The owner probably put them away for safekeeping."

For a moment, hope made him feel drunk with giddiness, but then he got a good look at her face. That cynical, world-weary look had returned, the look that said she believed the worst of people. "You don't believe that."

"No, I don't. But I need to be sure, so I'm going to wait for Mr. Dunn to return." She sat in one of the room's chrome chairs.

Christian needed to pace to siphon off his nervous energy, but the pain in his head would only increase with movement, so he sat in the other chair.

While they waited, Christian tried not to panic. The samples could be replaced. It would take a lot of work, and the suspects might not be so friendly and cooperative a second time. This was a minor setback, not a major catastrophe. He'd have to call Bryce as soon as they knew for sure.

By the time an older man walked into the office, Christian had calmed himself.

"I'm Harmon Dunn. Donny says you're looking for something from your Jeep?"

Christian stood. "There were two manila file folders full of evidence and a blueprint. Did you see them?"

"Sorry. I haven't been inside your car. Jeff moved it into the bay today. He helped steer it when the wrecker dropped it off yesterday. Otherwise, no one's been in your car."

"You'd better phone the police," Gabrielle said.

Mr. Dunn's eyebrows rose. "Why?"

Christian couldn't believe it. "I've been robbed."

CHAPTER 17

The police forensics specialist Gabrielle had insisted on finished dusting Christian's Jeep doors for fingerprints. Although she hoped otherwise, she was afraid whoever wanted Christian framed for the Densmore collapse hadn't left any prints. This case just kept getting stranger and stranger.

And her boss wasn't going to like this new turn of events. Somebody wanted his or her handwriting sample back, or they wanted to make the investigation murkier, or they just wanted to make sure Christian didn't present evidence to clear himself. Detective Bolling of the Highland Park police had questioned Gabrielle and Christian about the theft. He was fifty-something, growing thick through the middle, with short brown hair.

His partner, Detective Peterson, a thirty-something black man in a navy blue suit jacket entered from the garage bay. He glanced at Christian and her, then spoke to Bolling.

"There's been an odd development I think might be related. A company called DesignCorp in Highland Park had a break-in last night."

"DesignCorp?" Christian came to his feet. "Was anything taken?"

Peterson narrowed his eyes at Christian. "They had a small fire. In the records room."

"The Densmore records?" Gabrielle asked.

Peterson drilled her with a look. "They don't know what's destroyed yet. Highland Park PD is investigating."

"It can't be a coincidence," she said. "Not when our evidence is gone, too."

"Or you made sure all the so-called evidence disappeared," Bolling said. "Filing a false police report is a crime, Ms. Healey."

"Detective, someone is trying to erase what they did to make the Densmore collapse. Funny how that's happening now that Mr. Ziko and I are investigating. It sounds like someone is afraid we're going to find out the truth, doesn't it?"

"Can both of you account for your whereabouts last night?" Peterson asked.

"The press, who were camped outside Mr. Ziko's condo, can swear that we were there all night. Since Mr. Ziko has a concussion, I don't know how much time he can account for me. I know I can account for his whereabouts from around nine o'clock last night until this moment.

"We visited DesignCorp yesterday. Their connection to the Densmore design has been in the newspapers, so a smart person could put two and two together. I didn't see anyone following us yesterday, but I couldn't swear to it."

The forensics tech poked his head in the office. "I'll need Ms. Healey's prints. Mr. Ziko's are already on file."

After the police left, Christian called his lawyer and informed him about the lost evidence. When Christian disconnected the call, he told her, "Bryce says our request for dismissal has been denied."

"I'm sorry."

"Me too. I'd hoped it would be easy to prove I was innocent. So where does our investigation go from here? We can't go to Kernfelter, and DesignCorp is off limits. Bryce wants to see me when I have a chance."

"We'll have to retrace our steps and get signatures once again. Let's do it efficiently this time."

Christian barked a small laugh that stirred little flutters in Gabrielle's stomach. It was the first time she'd felt like smiling since he'd learned she was psychic. At the reminder, the flutters died and coldness took their place.

Together they made their plan. They set out for their first stop, calling to make sure Roger was in first.

*

It was a repeat of two days ago. Christian couldn't believe it had been only forty-eight hours, but so much had happened in the meantime. He glanced at Gabrielle as they exited the elevator on the top floor of the Piedmont Building. Her face showed no emotion. She must have plenty of experience hiding what she felt.

He hated being one more person to hurt her, but he couldn't cope with her psychic ability right now. He feared her touch, and what she might learn from it, which made him doubly careful of any incidental touching. He noticed she avoided him, too.

Brittany watched them approach and for the first time, he saw wariness in her eyes. He didn't blame her since he was forcing each of their employees under a cloud of suspicion. It wasn't easy to be treated like a suspect, to have someone doubt your word. He should know.

"Roger's in his office," Brittany said, her tone icy.

Roger's office was open. He looked up from the piles of paperwork on his desk. They didn't appear to have lessened in the days since they'd last been here.

"What do you want now, Kit?"

There was no softening what Christian had to say. "The handwriting samples were stolen. We need another one."

For a moment, Roger just looked at him. Then he threw down his pen. "Goddamit, I'm trying to run the business. If they were so goddamn important, why didn't you take better care of them?"

"I was in an accident and my car had to be towed. The samples were in the car."

Roger's face worked as he looked Christian over, his gaze fixing on the white bandage on Christian's forehead. "You were hurt?"

"Concussion."

"I'm sorry to hear that. I assume your concussion prevented you from doing any work for Barrett and Ziko?"

Christian was glad he'd worked last night while Gabrielle went to see her mother. "I made a dent in the pile you gave me."

Roger nodded, the lines around his mouth easing a little. He ran a hand through his thin hair, disarraying his perfect style. "But you're going to lose another day chasing handwriting samples instead of working?"

Christian chewed on his lip while he weighed his priorities. Gabrielle could pick up samples by herself—she didn't need him along for that. They'd asked their questions yesterday, so she wouldn't learn anything new today. While Roger needed his help a great deal. But it was his life, his freedom on the line. He needed to do this investigation with her.

"I should be available this afternoon to work on the rest of the projects I took home."

The remaining anger drained from Roger's face. When it was gone, Roger's face looked strained.

"The sample?" Gabrielle said.

Roger glared at her. "Hell." He grabbed a tablet and ripped off a sheet. After he scribbled furiously for several minutes, he handed the paper to them.

"Here. Take it and get the hell out of my office."

Christian took the sheet and headed for the door. Somehow this visit was just as detrimental on his and Roger's friendship as the first one had been. The only way he could see to mend the rift was to get Barrett and Ziko back on its feet again.

Retracing their steps to Brittany, Gabrielle slid a sheet of paper across to the receptionist.

"We need another sample of your handwriting," she said.

Brittany glared at Gabrielle. "I already did this."

"We need you to do it again," Christian said.

"It's not part of my job."

"Neither is screwing Paul Ziko," Gabrielle said.

Brittany paled, then her face suffused with red and her eyes narrowed. "Who told you that?"

"It doesn't matter. Just give us the sample."

"If it was true, and I'm not saying it is, what I do on my personal time is my own business."

Christian leaned closer to her. "Not when it involves subcontractors and not when it's my brother. My married brother."

She tossed her head. "People think just because I'm shaped the way I am that I sleep around." Her eyes slid to Gabrielle's smaller breasts with a sneer. "I think they're jealous."

"Just write." Christian had seen and sampled what Gabrielle had to offer and had been amply satisfied. Although he'd never made it with Brittany, he couldn't imagine being satisfied in bed with her. Not after he'd been one with Gabrielle.

Brittany snatched a pen from her desk and scribbled signatures on the paper. "There. If there's nothing else, Mr. Ziko, I have work to do. We all do here."

As Christian walked to the fax machine with Gabrielle following, he made a mental note to replace Brittany.

Gabrielle faxed the two samples to Kernfelter, and with a last glare from Brittany, they were on their way.

The difference between the two women was startling. He'd thought Brittany open and friendly, and Gabrielle reserved and secretive. Now he wondered if Brittany's friendliness was the false front, hiding at the very least the morals of an alley cat. Gabrielle's facade, on the other hand, protected a caring and passionate woman, easily hurt. She was secretive, but it was to protect herself. Of the two, he preferred the quiet depths of Gabrielle.

Christian tried Paul's cell phone on the way to the car, but got his voice mail. He left a message for his brother to contact him as soon as possible. A second call to Paul's office got a busy signal.

"Paul's not answering. Bryce's office is off 15 Mile in Sterling Heights."

Thunder rumbled off to the west. As Christian settled into the passenger seat, he remarked on it. "It's going to rain again."

"Then maybe we can catch half our suspects waiting in their cars for it to stop." She put the car in gear and headed for the freeway.

Christian didn't feel any easier going into Bryce's office today than he had yesterday. He almost wished Gabrielle had come in with him instead of waiting in the car. She said she'd get better cell phone reception outside, but he thought she wanted as much space between them as she could get for as long as she could get it.

Bryce looked as perfect and cold as he had the other day. "You want to tell me about the accident and your investigation?" It wasn't a question, even though it was phrased as one.

Christian gave him a rundown of everything that had happened. "Can you find out if all the Densmore records were destroyed?"

"I'll talk to the county prosecutor. DesignCorp has been subpoenaed to present the test results, so they'll have to provide some type of paperwork."

"Somebody doesn't want me cleared."

"It does seem too coincidental happening within hours of you beginning your investigation."

"If Gabrielle and I had used our heads, we could have faxed the signatures from each location. Then we might have a suspect."

Bryce's face had shown no emotion at all through Christian's tale. Now he sat back with his hands steepled in front of his chest. "Have you thought of anyone who might have done this to you?"

Christian sighed. "Before this week, I wouldn't have thought it of anybody. But now?" He ran his hands over his face. "Now there are a lot of people angry at me. I'm seeing people act in ways that disturb me. Even my secretary has become someone else. Hell, the brother of one of the people who died threatened me in front of the press yesterday."

"You sound disillusioned."

"Maybe I am. Gabrielle accused me of wearing rose-colored glasses. Not anymore."

"Don't fall apart on me."

A spurt of anger shot through Christian. "I won't. I'm not as fragile as you think."

"I hope not because we're going to trial the day after tomorrow."

Christian felt like he'd been speared in the gut. "What?"

Bryce leaned forward in his chair. "Your case has been pushed ahead. The mayor, city council, even the state senator want a fall guy for the Densmore. They think they'll get one with your trial."

Christian swallowed the nerves that threatened to rocket him right out of his chair. "Can't you ask for a delay or something? We need time to investigate."

"I already tried asking for a delay and was shot down."

"Are you ready?"

"I'd hoped to have another suspect from the handwriting samples. We need to point the finger of suspicion away from you. I don't know if Kernfelter's testimony alone will sway a jury."

Christian had to ask. "What are my chances?"

"I won't lie to you. Without another suspect, we're dependent on a sympathetic jury. But between the press coverage and the politicians rallying behind a reelection cause, we don't stand much chance of that."

Christian swallowed. After meeting with Kernfelter, he'd felt he had a chance. "Thanks for telling me." It was more imperative than ever that he find whoever was responsible. He didn't have a moment to waste.

He made his way out to the parking lot and slid into the rental car. "Did you reach anyone?"

"I left a message for Bryan Tuckerman. I've got an appointment with Hoepflmeier, Dortmouth and Cranston at one o'clock. But I still can't reach your brother. If we knew which job site he was at, we could just stop by there."

Thunder rumbled loudly overhead and Christian gritted his teeth. Paul was probably scrambling to get as much work done as possible before the next storm hit.

"My lawyer said we go to trial the day after tomorrow. There's political pressure to get a verdict. We're going to have to split up so we can interview everyone today."

"But you can't drive."

"I know. Bryce's secretary is finding me a limo service."

As they divided the suspects, the first sprinkles plopped fat and wet on the windshield. Christian would take the construction sites while trying to track down his brother through their mutual subcontractors. Gabrielle would tackle Christian's top competitors and the Republic Steel employee at his home. By the time they were finished, the rain had become a steady downpour. Bryan Tuckerman called and confirmed he was at the construction site in Warren waiting out the rain.

Then there was nothing left to plan. All that was left were words that had nothing to do with his innocence and everything to do with what lay between them.

"Gabrielle…"

"Don't. I need to get moving if we hope to have a case for you."

Damn it, there was so much to discuss, but now wasn't the time or place to do so. "Call me if you find out anything."

"I will."

Still Christian hesitated, staring into her face, willing her to look him in the eye, but she wouldn't. He climbed out into the rain and was soaked by the time he reached the foyer. He watched Gabrielle drive off, her taillights disappearing around the corner of the building, and he felt like he'd let something precious slip through his fingers.

CHAPTER 18

By the time Christian got Bryan Tuckerman's signatures, fat drops of rain splattered on the muddy ground around him, signaling the ten-minute reprieve was over. He left what cover the building frame provided and started carefully across the slick expanse of mud. As he headed past pallets of supplies, a rumble above him sounded like thunder, but then he caught movement from the corner of his eye. The stack of white PVC pipes tumbled down toward him.

Christian tried to leap out of the way, but slipped in the mud. As he fell on one knee, grunting with pain, he heard a shout. Then one of the PVCs slammed into his shoulder, knocking him sideways. He rolled to avoid the rain of heavy pipes. Their hollow thunder was deafening as they tumbled around him. Twice more he was struck, unable to avoid the cascade. He covered his head, hoping that would prevent serious injury. He kept his body small while the white pipes stacked up around him. Finally, the thunder ceased and blessed silence reined. He felt bruised and battered, but he was alive and none of the pipes had struck him in the head.

The shouts got louder and closer. PVC pipes were dragged from around him. Hands grabbed him and hauled him to his feet.

"Are you all right?" a man asked him.

Christian rotated his shoulder, wincing. "I think so."

"What happened?" someone shouted.

"PVC broke loose," another man said.

"Where's your hard hat?" a man resembling a drill sergeant asked.

"It's Christian Ziko," Bryan Tuckerman said, shouldering through the crowd. "He had business with me."

"You cursed or something, Ziko?" the big-chested man asked. "Do things collapse everywhere you go now?"

The group grew silent as slowly all of them looked from Christian to the top of the stacked pallets where the PVC pipe had been. Construction accidents happened all the time. People were in a hurry, they weren't careful, safety measures failed. But nothing had ever happened to Christian before. Two accidents in two days was too much coincidence for him. But could he prove the pipes weren't an accident?

In this rain, any evidence was probably washed away. But he had to start somewhere.

"Who's in charge here?" Christian asked.

"I am," the drill sergeant answered. "Take a break, you guys. We'll start working again as soon as the rain stops."

The construction workers drifted away toward their cars and trucks.

"I'm Mack McKenna," the other man identified himself. "I'm foreman here."

"I don't think this was an accident." Christian waved at the pipes on the ground. "I think somebody just tried to hurt me or worse."

"Nobody here knows you except Tuckerman."

"I don't think it was your crew. I think somebody followed me here and tried to take advantage of the rain."

"You've made a lot of enemies, Ziko. I'm one of them."

"I didn't do it. I've been investigating, trying to find out who did. Do you think the cops will be able to find any evidence in this rain?"

McKenna looked around the pallets and stared at the mud. "I doubt it. You want me to call them anyway?"

Christian sighed. The rain was soaking his clothes, and he shivered. Maybe it was chill, maybe shock that he'd come close to serious injury. "Let me contact my lawyer first. We can sit in my car while I make the call."

He scooped up the plastic portfolio, blessing Bryce's secretary for thinking of it. McKenna followed him to the limo, where the interior was blessedly quiet and dry. Christian speed dialed Bryce.

"Have you found something, Christian?" his lawyer asked when he came on the line.

"Someone just tried to kill me."

"What?" Bryce's voice snapped with unexpected emotion.

Christian described what happened, then added, "Bryce, I don't think the car accident yesterday was an accident."

"Shit."

"It seems like somebody doesn't want me to uncover the truth."

"You're sure it's not paranoid delusion?"

Christian sat straighter as anger burned through him. "Who told you that?"

"Paul called a little while ago. He thought you might be delusional."

"I'm not. I'll talk to you after the police get here."

When Christian explained the danger to the limo driver, the limo's owner wasn't willing to risk his property. The driver agreed to take Christian to the hospital to be checked for injuries. Christian called Gabrielle to pick him up at the hospital. When he hung up, a feeling of relief washed over him. He'd get to spend more time with her. It made no sense—he was afraid of her touch, but he still wanted her near.

CHAPTER 19

"I'm going to take a hot shower." Christian's gait was stiff and slow as he entered his condo in Bloomfield Hills. "Maybe that will make me feel better."

"I'll have your food ready in the kitchen." Gabrielle didn't want to think about him naked in the shower. That was the last place they'd been relatively happy. That had all changed when he'd found out she was psychic.

With the sound of the shower running, Gabrielle busied herself setting out the fast food they'd bought. While looking for dishes, she found three prescription bottles dated several days ago. Sean Bergman's name fairly jumped out at her from the labels. They were drugs she'd never heard of. What disease did he have that required three types of medication? All she could think of was AIDS. Remembering Christian making love to her without a condom caused her to break out in a cold sweat.

But he'd said he was clean, so it couldn't be AIDS. Transplant recipients and people with rheumatoid arthritis took lots of meds, but she'd seen him naked and there hadn't been any scars and his bones and joints looked fine. In fact, Christian appeared to be in great physical health. What could be wrong with him?

Whatever it was, it was his secret. Unless it affected the case… or her health.

Her hand itched to touch the bottles to learn the truth. But Christian was no longer the focus of her investigation. She didn't have the right to pry where he didn't want her to go. If they'd been in a relationship, she could ask him. But Christian was wary of her now.

A few minutes later, Christian came out of his bedroom carrying his muddy clothes. He'd put on clean blue jeans and a baby blue

Oxford shirt that deepened the blue of his eyes. When he passed her on his way to the laundry room, she couldn't help noticing how well the jeans hugged his firm buttocks, how long his slender legs looked in them. As he strode back toward her, she noted how his pants cupped his cock...and she was jealous. She knew what his clothes hid, and wanted to tear them off to get to the goods beneath. To hell with her stomach's hunger, she had other hungers that needed to be sated.

His blue eyes heated, noting the way she watched him approach. Was there anything sexier than an aroused man, one still damp from the shower? She wished she'd been there to lick the stray drops of water from his body.

Was it hot in here? She tore her gaze from his and stared at the island countertop. It was stupid to lust after his body when he'd made it clear he couldn't accept her completely.

Christian suggested in a thickened voice, "We could delay lunch."

Gabrielle looked into the darkened depths of his eyes. "I'd have to touch you."

He swallowed. "You've touched me before."

"You'd be completely open to me. I could learn anything you might not want me to know. I could learn what those pills in the cupboard are for."

His gaze snapped to the cupboard in question, now closed. He swallowed again. The flushed arousal in his cheeks faded. His gaze returned to her. "Did you...touch them?"

"I thought about it, but you said you weren't a risk to my health."

"I'm not."

"Are you a risk to me in any way because of those pills?"

He shook his head. "No."

"Do they have anything to do with the Densmore?"

Pain and then guilt darkened his eyes. The bottom dropped out of her stomach. What had he done?

When he spoke, his voice was strained. "I'm bipolar."

She couldn't have heard right. "What?"

"Bipolar. The medicine controls my mood swings, takes the tops off the highs, cuts the bottoms out of the lows."

Mood swings. He was a freakin' creative genius, of course he had them. A number of extremely creative people did. But there were some famous cases of those whose lows got too low, and when that happened...

Christian had disappeared after the Densmore collapsed. He had new medicine to control his moods. How severe had his low gotten? Had he overdosed or something? She'd seen the pain and desolation in his eyes when he looked at the Densmore. His pain ran deep. He felt too much.

She had to know. Was he a danger to himself and others? Had the car accident really been an accident or something darker?

She dragged the words through her tight throat, wanting to know the truth but afraid to ask. "Did you try to kill yourself?"

His tormented gaze jerked to hers. "No!"

"Where did you go after the Densmore collapsed?"

He looked away, but not before she saw the flash of guilt and the wasteland of hopelessness. It frightened her. "I committed myself to the Crittenden facility."

"Isn't that the rehab center where Detroit's rich and famous go to dry out?"

He nodded. "It also has a psychiatric wing. The staff is very discreet."

Discreet, right. "Sean Bergman is your psychiatrist?"

He nodded again.

"If you didn't try to kill yourself, why did you need Crittenden?"

"I...forgot...to take my medicine. Then I went too many days without it. I couldn't get out of bed. I couldn't function. I couldn't deal with the disaster. Paul took me to Crittenden and I signed myself in."

With every word, he appeared to be crumbling inside. Gabrielle feared a relapse. Her voice was sharp when she demanded, "Have you had your medication today?"

"Yes, damn it. I know better now than to skip a day. I'm not going to fall apart. I wish everyone would stop doubting me. I'm not going to let it happen again, ever."

God, the hurt rolled off him in waves. She needed so badly to touch him, to make him stop hurting.

But when she reached for him, he recoiled. "Trying to see if I'm telling the truth?"

She jerked back as though he'd struck her. "No. I sensed your pain..."

His eyes widened. "But you didn't even touch me."

"Even non-psychics can read body language and facial expressions."

"Oh." Some of the rigidity went out of his spine.

"How long have you been bipolar?"

"The doctors said probably since puberty. A lot of...mental illnesses...show up at puberty and in the teen years."

"But you aren't sure when yours started?"

Christian looked away. "I didn't have trouble until my parents died."

Gabrielle put two and two together and came up with a scene similar to or worse than after the Densmore incident. "Were you hospitalized then?"

He nodded. "I was a minor so Paul committed me."

And because of his illness he'd stayed by Paul ever since. His much older brother had built for him a safe haven surrounded by friends loyal to Paul. In this cocoon, Paul could be sure Christian would not have a relapse.

But Paul couldn't have foreseen the Densmore.

"Why don't you eat your lunch so we can see Cranston's partner and then the Republic Steel employee?" she said.

Lunch was a silent, stilted affair. She felt Christian's glances, questioning, accusing, disturbed. He should be more accepting in light of his own condition.

She drove to the offices of Hoepflmeier, Dortmouth and Cranston Architects in Warren, where Christian agreed to wait in the lobby. They felt fairly certain no one would attempt anything here since the wall of glass that separated the lobby from the outer corridor prevented anyone from sneaking up on the lobby occupants.

Ted Hoepflmeier, the gray-haired man she'd seen in her vision with Bob Cranston, rose from behind his cherry wood desk when she entered his office.

Gabrielle held out her hand and introduced herself.

When the sixty-something Hoepflmeier clasped it, the vision burst into her brain.

"Barrett and Ziko won the Rothberger bid, Al." Hoepflmeier slid a letter in front of another man close to his age, who must be the other partner, Allen Dortmouth.

"Damn it, not another one." Al pounded a fist onto the letter. "We've got to do something about them."

Hoepflmeier waved to the letter. "Him, not them. It's Ziko's designs that are winning, not Barrett's."

Al shifted his gaze from the letter to his partner. "Have you tried hiring him?"

Al shook his head. "He's tied too closely to Barrett through his brother. He won't leave the firm."

"We can't just let him continue to snap up all the projects in town."

"No, we can't."

The vision dissolved. Gabrielle could scream at the bait being dangled in front of her and then being yanked away. She needed the rest of that discussion. What had the senior partners decided to do about Christian?

Hoepflmeier waved her to a cherry wood and leather chair in

front of his desk. "My partner, Bob Cranston, told me about your meeting yesterday. I didn't expect you to come here. What do you want, Ms. Healey?"

Gabrielle explained about investigating the disaster, then added, "Do you know anyone at Barrett and Ziko?"

"I know both principals. I make it a point to know my competition." His eyes showed the crafty businessman inside.

"Anyone else there?"

"No, why?"

"I wondered how familiar you were with your competition. Do any of your employees socialize with any of Barrett and Ziko's?"

"I wouldn't know. I don't pry into my employees' social lives."

Gabrielle decided to use a more direct approach. "How would you benefit if something happened to Barrett and Ziko?"

His gray eyes narrowed. "Are you making accusations, Ms. Healey?"

"No, just trying to determine how the Densmore accident affected your firm."

"It didn't. We didn't design it or build it. We're not culpable in any way."

"How closely do you work with DesignCorp?"

Hoepflmeier's expression wiped from his face. "As closely as every other architectural firm in this city." He rose. "I think we're done here."

"Thanks for your time. I know my way out." Gabrielle left his office and returned to the lobby. She placed a finger over her lips and signaled Christian outside.

Beyond the competition's hearing, she filled him in on what little she'd found out. "They wanted to stop you, but I couldn't find out what they'd done, if anything."

Christian pushed the button for the elevator. "That doesn't do us any good. Why didn't you find out the rest?"

"It doesn't work that way. It's not like a TV remote where I can tune in any channel I want. Did you give their names to your lawyer?"

"Yeah. I gave him a list of our major competitors. But we can't go into court with a list of competitors as suspects."

The elevator opened and they stepped inside, just them and their hostility. Gabrielle explained what happened. "I did what I could. We might have had more luck if we hadn't run into Cranston yesterday. He told his partner and Hoepflmeier was ready with his answers."

"You should have thought of that yesterday."

Gabrielle had had enough. She didn't have to defend herself. "If you don't like the way I'm investigating, you can call a cab and go home."

Outside the gray overcast sky was as depressing as their conversation.

"I'm not giving up until I clear my name," Christian said.

As they approached the car in the visitor's lot, she saw the flat tire.

"Damn, the tire's flat." She hoped the rental was equipped with a spare.

"Gabrielle."

The odd note in Christian's voice pulled her gaze toward the front of the car. That tire was flat too.

"What the hell?"

Christian crouched by the back tire, wincing as he did so. "This has been slashed."

Striding around the other side of the car, she found those tires slashed as well. "This side too."

The back of her neck prickled. She whirled, sure she was being watched. But she saw no one in the parking lot. Scanning the glass walls of the building that housed Cranston and his partners, she didn't see anyone standing at the window looking down on them from the sixth floor. But someone had targeted Christian twice already.

"Christian, get down!"

As he spun a startled face toward her, she bounded around the tail of the car and blocked him with her body from where she thought someone might be hiding.

"What is it?" He tried to get around her.

"I feel like someone's watching. Don't you?"

"We're in a parking lot. There are plenty of people coming and going."

"Christian, wake up. Somebody doesn't want you poking your nose into this investigation. We're standing here in the open in front of a competitor who'd rather see you out of business. You couldn't be a bigger target right now. Let's go back inside."

"To the competitor?"

"No, to the lobby."

Gabrielle took hold of his arm, ignoring his slight flinch. The vision was harder to ignore.

Christian lay on what looked like a floor. He'd slashed his wrist open. The scarlet that flowed over his tanned skin was frightening.

Christian tore his hand from Gabrielle's. He'd paled and his jaw bunched with some dark emotion. Had he seen the vision too?

He kept his distance from her as they entered the lobby. The vision had been foresight, which was becoming the norm instead of the exception around him. He'd said he wasn't suicidal, but the vision indicated otherwise.

As he whipped out his cell phone, she stared at his unscarred wrist. Would this investigation drive him to kill himself? And how could she prevent it from happening? In the vision she hadn't been there, which was odd, since she and Christian had spent the past two days together.

CHAPTER 20

"You've sure stirred up a hornet's nest," Bryce Gannon said when Christian finished telling him about the car tires being slashed. "It's a clear message somebody wants you to stop."

"But I'm not going to."

"Why slash the tires, though? If they want you out of commission, why not use a car bomb?"

"Geez, Bryce, that's a cheerful thought."

"It makes no sense. Why the car and not you?"

"I don't know. If it's someone at Hoepflmeier, Dortmouth and Cranston, why do something in their own parking lot?"

"Maybe they're stupid. Hell, I don't know. I'll call the Warren PD again and ask for the same detective."

After he hung up, Christian found Gabrielle waiting near the outer door.

"Enterprise is sending a tow truck and another car," she said.

"Bryce is calling the cops."

She held up a hand. "Wait here. I want to check something out before the cops arrive." She pushed the door open.

"Where are you going?"

"To investigate. I'll be right back. I don't think they're after me."

Christian hated having to be careful while Gabrielle pursued the truth.

Only a few minutes passed before she returned. "Brittany slashed the tires. She was dressed in coveralls and a ball cap, but I could tell by her figure."

Christian shook his head. "But she drives a red Mazda. It was a dark SUV that ran me into the barrier yesterday."

156

"I think she's working with somebody else. She had no reason to alter the drawing herself. Someone must have asked her to do it, or bribed her, or coerced her in some way."

"I can't picture someone coercing her." Now that he'd seen she wasn't all sweetness and light.

"I think it more likely that she traded sex for it or she did it out of spite. She seems that kind of woman."

He'd worked with Brittany for a year and never noticed that about her. Was it because Gabrielle was also a woman that she saw Brittany for the person she really was? Then something else she'd said sunk in.

"And you think it's Paul because she slept with him?" It couldn't be Paul.

"I think a woman like her knows how to use her body to get what she wants. Your brother is probably one of many to fall for her ploys. I think your partner slept with her, too."

"So we tell the police it was Brittany?" he asked.

"Um, it's not that easy. We have to have proof."

"But you saw her."

Gabrielle grimaced. "Not with my eyes."

Oh. Christian realized he'd believed her about Brittany without reservation. How had he gone from being dismayed about her psychic abilities to accepting it as an investigative tool?

He thought of another difficulty. "What if she didn't leave fingerprints? We can't let her get away with what she did."

"We'll tell the police we have suspicions it was her and ask them to check her alibi."

Christian dug out his phone and dialed his office, only to find out from Roger that Brittany was on an errand.

After he hung up, Gabrielle was livid with him. "Roger slept with Brittany. If he tells her about the call, she'll know we're on to her. We need to keep the element of surprise on our side. What were you thinking?"

Frustration welled up like bitter acid. "I was thinking I worked with honest people. I don't want to believe I'm surrounded by people I can't trust. I'll go crazy if I do."

"It's probably only two people, with at least one of them inside your company. I doubt it's a large conspiracy."

"That doesn't make me feel better." Was he such a poor judge of character? It was galling and frightening at the same time.

It was no surprise when the police didn't find any fingerprints on the rental car. Then Christian and Gabrielle had to waste an hour at the police station filling out a report. Christian was still fuming as they navigated Jerry Flanders's residential neighborhood in Dearborn.

There they learned the former Republic Steel rep had dealt directly with Paul Ziko, and that Paul had given him the length substitution. Jerry was appalled the difference had caused the Densmore's collapse.

When they were back in the car, Christian waited only until the door closed to exclaim, "Paul isn't guilty. He went back to Roger and someone there changed the drawing."

"At Paul's insistence."

"No. He wouldn't do that to me."

"It's business, Christian. If you can't afford one material, you try to substitute another."

"But those girders weren't interchangeable. It had to be that length."

"Exactly."

Christian gritted his teeth. His brother wouldn't have done that, couldn't have. He'd known Paul for thirty-two years. He'd never done anything to hurt Christian.

But now he'd tried to tell Christian's doctor how to treat him, and Christian's lawyer how to handle his case. He'd wanted Christian to return to Crittenden to avoid prosecution for the Densmore.

No, that was his big brother trying to do what he'd always done and smooth Christian's way. There was nothing underhanded in what Paul had done.

"Christian, you've got to admit to the possibility."

"He's my brother. Until I see more than speculation, I'm going to believe he's innocent. Show me some proof."

"I don't have it yet. But if he were anyone else, we'd dig for a connection with someone at your firm, and we wouldn't stop until we knew who it was. With your brother, not only is Roger his best friend but we know he and Brittany were having an affair."

"How did their having sex suddenly become a plan to substitute material on the Densmore? I don't see her getting anything out of the Densmore's collapse. Paul either, for that matter."

"He built the Densmore within the budget and he got to keep the Densmore project," she said.

"We wouldn't have taken it away from him." He noted they were heading south. "Where are we going?"

"We're fifteen minutes from my house. If you feel up to it, I'd like to stop there and you can take the rental car home."

He was feeling a lot better, but he didn't want to go home alone. The thought of spending a long evening with his doubts left him cold.

By the time she pulled into the driveway of a small, older home, he still hadn't figured out a way to stay. But his perusal of her neat, well-cared-for home was cut short by the half dozen people converging on the car with camcorders, lights and microphones.

"Looks like a welcoming party," he said.

"It has to be related to the Densmore investigation, but how do they know you're with me?"

"I don't know. Do you want to go to my condo?"

She shook her head and sighed. "No. I'm sure reporters are there, too." She opened her door.

Immediately, a reporter stuck a microphone in front of her. "Ms. Healey, is it true that you can predict the future?"

Christian saw Gabrielle stiffen.

Her voice was crisp when she answered. "I perform a fortune teller act at parties. I play a part."

"Then you're not a psychic?" another reporter asked.

A muscle in her jaw bunched. "Excuse me." She slid out of her seat and stood.

"Are you a psychic, Ms. Healey?" the reporter insisted.

Christian had exited the car as well. He wondered why Gabrielle didn't tell them the truth, until he remembered she didn't want anyone to know, especially her employer. She looked like a fox surrounded by baying hounds.

He strode around the car and took hold of her arm. Immediately he was swamped by a vision of plunging his cock into the warmth between Gabrielle's spread legs. Her snug wet body gloved him perfectly. As he withdrew slightly, her hips rose to receive his thrust.

Oh no, they weren't going to share this vision in front of the press. He urged her toward her front door. Reporters threw questions at them as they moved.

"Did you predict the Densmore collapse, Ms. Healey?"

"Are you using your psychic abilities to investigate the collapse?" one yelled.

"Are you the only psychic at Michigan Casualty, or are there others?" another asked.

"Ms. Healey hasn't said she's a psychic. If you'll excuse us." Christian followed Gabrielle through the door and closed it behind him.

Gabrielle looked shell-shocked. "I'm going to lose my job."

"No you're not. You didn't admit anything."

"I don't have to admit it. They're going to air their allegations and convict me in the press. At the very least, I'll be taken off the Densmore case. At the most, I'll lose my job. Insurance is a conservative industry. Why did I let you tag along with me?

I knew it was a bad idea. You're in the spotlight. Some of it was bound to spill over onto me."

He took hold of her elbow. Immediately, he was inundated by the vision.

"Don't touch me." She shook him off.

"This is a vision of the future. Tonight. We both want to experience again what we shared last night."

She shook her head. "You're uncomfortable with my abilities."

"I shared them a moment ago, and all the way in from the car."

"You don't mind those visions, but if I asked you to allow me to hold your pill bottles or touch your bed in order to learn more about you, you wouldn't be comfortable."

No, he wouldn't be. He didn't like her plumbing his secrets from touching the material things in his life. Those secrets were his to tell or keep. His choice, not hers.

Christian tried to explain. "I'm still unnerved that you know things I don't want you to know, but it hasn't even been twenty-four hours since I found out."

Gabrielle looked uncertain and more than a little wary. If they could experience the oneness they'd shared last night, he was sure it would ease both their doubts. So he reached for her, knowing they'd be swamped by the vision.

At the touch of her silky skin, the vision washed over them and swept them into a vortex of passion. He found her lips and opened his over hers. Her tongue pushed into his mouth, found his. That small touch fanned the flames. He clasped her to him tightly.

Her body pressed to his echoed the vision where they were already naked and yearning toward completion. For a moment, he wished to be able to make love to Gabrielle without visions urging him faster. He wanted to savor the feel of her lips and her body. He wanted to linger at the joint where her neck met her collarbone, or where her thigh met her body. He needed to spend time adoring her curves, tasting what made her unique and feminine.

But this wasn't that time. Already Gabrielle cupped his buttocks, pressing the front of him into the vee of her legs. Her breasts were crushed to his chest. He wanted them in his palms instead. As she made yearning thrusts against him, he tried to maneuver them toward something soft.

"Bed?" was all he could get out before she claimed his lips again.

They were moving, but he couldn't tell if Gabrielle was trying to reach the front of his pants, or if he was maneuvering to be able to touch her breasts. His back bumped the wall, then Gabrielle was all over him. She shoved a hand down the front of his pants to caress his cock. She slid her other hand up his chest under his shirt, rubbing his pecs and nipples.

All he seemed able to do was breathe, and that was difficult. She fondled the length of him, and then dug deeper into his pants to cup his balls. He threw his head back, whacked the wall behind him and saw stars. He groaned, both from the pain of it and from the pleasure she was giving him as she rubbed.

"Sorry," she said.

He grabbed her forearms and turned her so her back was to the wall. She dragged him to her, eliciting a groan from him.

Two could play at this game. Unbuttoning her shirt, he slid the cotton off her shoulders, where it caught on her upper arms. He unlatched her bra's front catch and flicked the lacy cups open. He had a moment to marvel over the bronze tips before he covered them with his hands. He molded the firm, silky globes, feeling the hardened tips press into his palms.

"Perfect."

"Almost," she said. "It would be better in bed."

"I don't know where your bedroom is." Then he kissed her, open-mouthed and completely carnal.

Her lips tasted like the headiest wine, and he was intoxicated. Holding her plump breasts in his hands, he felt like he held the world, held all possibilities. Only one thing could make this moment with her better.

She pressed forward against him, directing him to his right. He went willingly, although slowly. Any faster speed was difficult while Gabrielle's hand was down the front of his pants. But his movements forced her hand to exert harder pressure on his penis. He groaned into her mouth, hoping they made it to the bed in time. He wanted to be inside her when he came.

She slid her tongue across his and explored the inside of his mouth. He bit her tongue lightly and then sucked on it.

Gabrielle growled and pushed against him. The back of his legs hit something, and he toppled over, dragging her down on top of him. They landed on the bed with an oomph.

Before he could catch his breath, Gabrielle wrenched on the snap of his jeans. She nearly did him damage dragging down the zip. He inhaled to give her more room. In seconds, she'd bared him.

He helped her push her pants down her hips. Then she kicked them off. He grabbed a condom from the pocket of his jeans. Gabrielle took it, sheathed him, and then she was over him. He helped her sink down on his eager shaft, sheathing himself where he most wanted to be. They both groaned with relief. He was almost there, to the point they'd shared several times last night.

Their vision selves were drenched with sweat, holding off orgasm by sheer willpower. He was so hard in real life, he didn't know why he didn't come as soon as Gabrielle mounted him.

But Christian wanted to extend the moment. He didn't want their loving to be a race against visions in their heads. He thrust, measuring his length inside her body. He reached up to cup her beautiful breasts in his hands. She arched into him while she ground her body down on him.

They were a perfect match. Her body was made solely for his. They made love together, meeting and separating and doing it over again. As though they'd been lovers for years instead of days, their thrusts were perfectly timed. Although his loins burned with the need to come, he wouldn't until they could do it together.

"Christian."

"Call me Kit."

"Kit. This feels so good."

"Yeah, it does." Sex had never felt so right. Beyond animal passion, beyond physical pleasure, the sense of belonging overwhelmed him. He should lay claim to this woman, so he had the right to do this with her every day for the rest of their lives.

He reached one of his hands between their thrusting bodies, and caressed her clitoris with a finger.

Gabrielle moaned and then stiffened as her inner contractions began. He let go of his barely there control then, following her over into the place where she and he had no end. Their halves fused and he felt complete again. Warmth spread through him.

She collapsed onto him and he caressed her long back with a possessive hand. If he had his way, there would never be another woman in his life, in his bed. How could there be when he was a part of the woman lying on top of him. He'd never look at his secretary again and admire her curves.

Gabrielle lifted her head, frowning. Her blue eyes, still dilated with passion, were confused. "Why were you thinking about Brittany just now?"

"Jesus Christ." His whole body stiffened. Then he rolled her off him and bounded out of the bed. The sweat cooled on his body, making him shiver as he stood staring down at her. That she'd picked that little tidbit out of his mind scared him half to death. "You swore you didn't read minds."

"I don't."

"You just did." Had what they'd shared made him an open book to her? He didn't want her reading his mind. Was she doing it even now? He couldn't reason over his racing heart.

She narrowed her eyes, and her face reddened. Snatching the sheet, she covered her body with it. "I read people. I happened to pick up that."

"You took it right out of my mind. God." He ran a hand through his hair. "I can't do this." He had to reflect on what had happened and what it meant. But he couldn't do that here.

Grabbing his clothes, he hastily threw them on.

"You're just going to leave?"

"I'm going home to think." He was babbling.

"I see."

"I don't think you do." He finished dressing, tried to straighten his hair and then turned for the doorway. Hesitating, he wondered if they could talk it over, and maybe she could make him understand. But he'd been soul-bound with her one minute and then she'd read his mind the next. A soul he could share, but his mind… God, he didn't know.

"I'll call you." He headed for the front door and escape.

Reporters mobbed him all the way to the car, but he didn't say one word. How could he, when those words would be, "Yes, she's a psychic." Wouldn't they love to hear she was also telepathic?

CHAPTER 21

The front door slam as Christian ran from her house was like a death knell to Gabrielle. She didn't believe he'd be back. He'd been freaked this morning when he found out she was psychic, but he'd needed her to help him investigate. So he'd stayed with her all day. Then, when the fright had subsided, he thought he'd get more sex.

She should have kept her mouth shut. She should have known she'd receive all kinds of images lying on top of him with his body inside hers. All his defenses had been down, so he'd been like an open book. They'd achieved the same oneness they had this morning, and so she couldn't understand why he'd be thinking of another woman.

But she'd frightened him. Christian's blue eyes had been huge after she asked about Brittany. He'd fairly flown out of bed he couldn't get away from her fast enough. He'd taken an emotional beating the past few weeks, losing his beliefs one by one, and he couldn't handle any more.

Gabrielle hugged herself, feeling chilled. She didn't want to get out of bed, but Christian leaving meant the front door was unlocked. She wouldn't feel safe from the press until the locks were set.

As she rose from the bed, something on the carpet caught her eye. It was the condom they'd used. She bent to pick it up, hysterical laughter bubbling up in her throat. She'd shriveled him so fast the condom had fallen off his limp penis. She'd given a new meaning to frigid.

Gabrielle caught back a sob. *Don't. You knew better than to get involved.* And yet some foolish part of her hoped he'd call her and apologize. How stupid was that?

She knew the truth. It was her heart talking, her heart that had wanted her father to come back home and love her, that had dreamed a college sweetheart would end up her husband, that hoped yin and yang were permanent.

Had she fallen in love with him? She scoffed. What did she know of love? Her grandmother had sternly taught her what it meant to have a gift like hers.

But Christian had taught her something else. He'd taught her to care whether someone else was happy, to yearn to offer comfort and solace, to delight in the smile on their face. She'd seen his pain over the trouble with the people he loved, and she'd felt a burning desire to not see his life destroyed. She wanted to help him, be with him, work side by side with him, and make love with him.

And for only the second time in her life, she thought about giving a man children. That meant passing on her gift to another generation. Another little girl blessed or cursed with the sight. She was sure a child of hers would be clairvoyant.

She'd showered and changed into cotton shorty pajamas when the phone rang. Her heart leaped into her throat pounding madly. He'd called.

Part of her held back from snatching the phone from the cradle. What if it wasn't him? She concentrated, but couldn't get a read on who the caller was. Nothing new there—her gift was for something else.

But as she touched the phone, she knew the caller was her boss, Cal Beyers. What did he want? A glance at her watch showed it was nearly seven o'clock, way past quitting time. And he was calling her home phone. There was only one way to find out what he wanted.

"Hello?"

"Gabrielle, it's Cal."

"Hi, Cal. You're calling late."

"I saw the local news and I'm disturbed."

Damn it. She sank to the bed and forced an unfelt smile. "Disturbed about what?"

"The news said you might be psychic."

Gabrielle's hand tightened on the phone. She took a breath to calm herself before answering. "Did they also report it's an act I perform at parties?"

"I don't understand why you were telling fortunes."

"Look, Cal, I'm entitled to have a second job and to do what I want at that job. With my hair color, I can easily play the part of a gypsy. It's easy money, it's fun to do, and I'm not hurting anybody. And it doesn't interfere with my day job."

"The speculation about a psychic's involvement in Ziko's snooping puts Michigan Casualty in a bad light. I got a call from senior management a little while ago. They're nervous. Frankly, so am I. We don't need bad publicity, not on top of the Densmore calamity. I told you to steer clear of Ziko and bring in a ruling in our favor. Do you intend to do that, or should we consider you a liability, in light of tonight's publicity?"

She ground her back teeth together. She couldn't lie, nor could she tell the truth. She couldn't give in, yet she couldn't lose her job either.

"There's been a development. Someone tried to kill Christian Ziko twice."

"What?" Cal nearly shouted the word.

"Once yesterday and once today. He goes to trial in thirty-six hours, but someone wants him silenced, and the investigation stopped. Someone wants to make sure he stays guilty, that he never makes it to trial." She shut up and waited.

Cal was silent a long time. Finally, he spoke. "I'm going to give you enough rope to hang yourself. You've got thirty-six hours. If your report isn't on my desk at eight a.m. the day after tomorrow, you can consider yourself terminated. I don't want anyone working for me who won't follow orders."

Gabrielle swallowed. She hoped her voice didn't quake when she answered. "I understand."

"I hope you do. I'd planned to recommend you to senior management to replace me. Instead, I have to note this verbal warning. Good-night." The line went dead without Cal waiting for an answer.

Gabrielle dropped the phone back onto the base. Her hands trembled wildly. She was going to lose her job. She and Christian had interviewed all the suspects and hadn't pinpointed anyone for sure. They had suspicions, but no hard facts or evidence. How could she turn in a final report when she didn't know who was guilty?

It was time to visit her mother, but in her agitated state, she wouldn't be a calming influence on her parent. Besides, with the press out front, she didn't want them following her to the nursing home. She picked up the phone again to call the nursing home. This evening was just full of disappointments.

*

Christian pulled into his driveway nearly an hour after he left Gabrielle's house. The freeway had been bumper to bumper all the way home. He'd crawled past two accidents that had traffic tied up in snarls.

His head throbbed, although he was afraid it was from the tension of leaving Gabrielle and gritting his teeth on the freeway. He shouldn't have left her like that. It was too abrupt. But he'd felt like the hounds of hell were after him, afraid she'd probe his thoughts without even touching him. After all, hadn't he become one with her?

Unable to turn around on the freeway due to heavy traffic, he'd suffered through alternating attacks of conscience and fear. What would it mean to be with a woman and never have any privacy?

She'd know if he looked at a pretty woman, know if someone made a pass at him, know secrets other people told him in confidence. It wasn't only his secrets she'd be able to pry out of his mind.

He'd never be able to throw a surprise party, buy her a gift she didn't know about in advance or be able to hide her Christmas presents. How could there be spontaneity if there couldn't be surprise?

Reporters were parked in the street outside his condo. Damn. They converged on his car as he was getting out. But past them one man drew his attention: Wes Masterson leaned against the side of his condo, his eyes glaring his hatred even from this distance. Christian wasn't up to this after the scene with Gabrielle and the self-flagellating drive home.

"Mr. Ziko, is it true Gabrielle Healey is a psychic?"

"Why did you hire a psychic?"

"I hear someone tried to kill you today."

Christian's head jerked toward the third reporter. "Who told you that?"

"I have sources in the Warren PD. So it's true?"

"Yes," Christian admitted. Maybe if they printed the truth, whoever was after him would stop because they were worried about getting caught.

"Who tried to kill you?" another reporter asked.

"I don't know yet."

"Where's Ms. Healey?" someone shouted.

"She's at home." There was less than ten feet to his door and Wes Masterson.

Wes looked even angrier than he had last evening. He straightened away from the house as Christian approached. "Don't think you're going to get away with killing my sister and the others by hiring someone to make it look like you're in danger. We all know the truth. You're guilty. You murdered those people. No one's trying to kill you, Ziko, at least not actively."

"I didn't kill your sister."

"You sure as hell did and you're going to pay for it. I'm going to make sure of it."

Christian felt so tired of fighting everyone. He couldn't fight people's thoughts, and they seemed happy to think the very worst about him. He reached past Wes to insert the key in the lock, but Wes grabbed his arm.

"I know what you're up to, but it's not going to work. No one's going to believe a piece of crap like you, a killer."

Christian shook his arm loose and forced the key into the lock. But he tried one last time with Wes. "I didn't kill your sister."

Wes stalked away and Christian closed the door on the shouting reporters. He couldn't take any more questions when they didn't want to listen to his answers.

When his cell phone rang he didn't feel like answering. If it was Gabrielle, what would he say to her? But the caller ID showed Paul's number, so he flipped open the phone. "Paul, where have you been? I've been calling you all day."

"Is it true? Is she a psychic?"

"Gabrielle?"

"Don't try to play dumb, little brother. I heard it on the news. Is that how she knew about me and Brittany?"

Christian sighed. "Yes."

"What the hell are you doing? Do you want people to think you're crazy? First Crittenden, now you're using a psychic?"

"I'm not crazy and Gabrielle just happens to be psychic in addition to being an investigator."

"Sure. She just happens to be psychic. What, are you using her as a human lie detector?" Paul's voice was sharp with disdain.

"Paul, I'm just trying to find out the truth. I go on trial the day after tomorrow."

Paul sucked in his breath. "My God, so soon?"

"Yes. If you'd called me back, I would have told you."

"I've been busy. I've got six major jobsites going at once and they all need my attention." Paul's voice showed the strain.

"What happened to your assistant?" Christian asked.

"It doesn't matter."

"What happened to her?"

"I had to lay her off, all right?" Paul said. "Money's tight and I couldn't afford to pay her. It's been a bad year."

Christian scrubbed his face. "Jesus, Paul. You didn't tell me."

"I don't tell you my problems, Kit. I take care of you, not the other way around."

Christian stood straighter. "Maybe it's time that changed. I'm a grown man now."

"You're my baby brother. You're always going to be my responsibility."

Christian clenched his fist in frustration. He had to show Paul he didn't need looking after any more. "Paul, we talked to Jerry Flanders at Republic Steel today. He said you changed the order to twenty-five-foot girders for the Densmore."

"I couldn't get the thirty footers. I bought what I could afford. It happens all the time."

"But the drawing doesn't work with the shorter length. Who'd you ask to change the drawing?"

"Roger, of course."

That jived with what Roger had said. Another dead end. "Bro, we need another sample of your handwriting. Can you come over now?"

"No, I've got a meeting in a few minutes about problems at one of my sites. I don't know how long it will last."

"How about first thing tomorrow?"

"Sure. I don't know where I'll need to go first, but I'll call you and let you know where to meet me."

"Okay."

"But don't bring that psychic," Paul said. "I don't have much that's private from you, but I'd prefer she not know everything about me and tell you."

Christian knew how Paul felt. "I understand."

"I don't know how you've stood being around her these past few days."

"I didn't know."

"She kept that on a need-to-know basis?"

Now Paul wanted Christian to spill Gabrielle's secrets. Christian was just as uncomfortable doing that as he'd been knowing Gabrielle was reading him. "It's complicated."

"I'll bet. Does she know about Crittenden?"

Christian sighed. "Yeah."

"Kit, you know she'll put it in her report and make you look guilty."

He'd wondered if she considered that 'off the record' because they'd slept together. Or was everything he did and said still part of the investigation? No, Gabrielle wouldn't do that. But she'd kept a major investigative tool secret from him. Maybe she was capable of that.

"I don't think she would."

"Kit, trust me on this. You're naïve about people. If it comes to a choice between spilling your secrets or her job, she's going to choose the job. I'm the only one you can trust completely. Listen to me."

A lifetime of listening to his brother's good advice kicked in. Paul had never steered him wrong before. But Paul hadn't slept with Gabrielle, hadn't fused himself to her soul. However, Christian couldn't tell his brother that because Paul would think Christian had been swayed by sex. He wouldn't understand.

"I have to go, Paul. I'll see you tomorrow."

"Think about what I said, little brother."

Long after Christian hung up, he thought about Gabrielle and her ability to read his mind. She'd touched him that first day, at the Densmore. What had that touch told her? At that point, she hadn't slept with him, so her loyalty had been to her job. What had she learned and had she reported it to her employer? Were most of his thoughts and feelings written down somewhere in her file on the Densmore?

He shuddered. He wanted to shout his denial, but they'd only been intimate for twenty-four hours. He knew very little about her, other than that he considered her his soulmate. He couldn't say how she'd react in any situation. His heart and his mind were at odds, and he felt more lost now than when his parents died. Thank God he had his brother to hold onto.

*

The phone's strident ring dragged Gabrielle from an uneasy sleep where she'd dreamed of Christian in need but had been unable to reach him.

Grabbing the receiver, she hauled it to her mouth. "Hello?"

"What the hell were you thinking?" Christian shouted.

"Huh?"

"Did you do it to hurt me? I told you I needed time. Jesus, you couldn't even wait twelve hours."

A glance at the clock showed it was a little after seven a.m. "What are you talking about?"

"You know damn well what I'm talking about."

Gabrielle pushed herself to a sitting position. "No, actually, I don't."

"The *Detroit Free Press* story about me and Crittenden. Why'd you tell them?"

That cleared the fog from Gabrielle's brain. "I didn't tell anybody anything."

"You're the only one I told, and that was in confidence."

"I repeat, I didn't tell anybody anything."

"It's here in black and white. Reporters have been calling me for the past half hour demanding to know why I was there."

"What'd you tell them?"

"No comment. There's no way I'll admit to the truth. But that story is pretty damaging. Why'd you do it?"

He wasn't going to believe her. He thought she'd sold him out. Well, this was a new twist. Usually men lied to her.

Her breath backed up in her throat. Was this Christian's answer then? Was this his way of pushing her out of his life? It had to be. Their time together meant nothing, when stacked against her gift.

It hurt. It hurt terribly. And she struck back to wound. "I'm no coward. If I'd done it, I would admit it to you. Unlike you, who can't even tell me the truth that you're afraid to be with me because I'm psychic. No, you have to make up some lie about me talking to the press in order to dump me. You retreat every time something unusual happens in your safe little world, tucking your head in just like a turtle. Well that's no way to live—in fact, that's not living at all."

She hung up on Christian's sputtering. Tears threatened to spill from her eyes. Damn it, she was no virgin to heart wars. She should have been awarded the Purple Heart each time a man had inflicted wounds on her psyche and her soul. She was unwanted. Why couldn't she accept that? Why did she keep putting her heart on the line? No one could love someone like her. Why was she surprised?

Because I love him.

Fool. Stupid fool.

As she sniffed back a sob that threatened to tear her apart, the phone rang again. Her foolish heart leaped, hoping against hope that Christian was calling to apologize. But the caller ID listed Cal Beyers's name.

She didn't want to talk to him, either, but he'd know she was home. He must have seen the story. Shit.

"Hello, Cal."

"Did you know about Ziko and Crittenden?"

What could she say? What should she say? There was no right answer. "He mentioned it."

"And you didn't think it was important? A private rehab facility where the crème of the city go to dry out, and you didn't think it had any bearing on the case?"

Oh God. She hadn't known the *Free Press* had put that spin on it. But there was no way she could correct Cal's perception without spilling Christian's secret. Despite what Christian thought, she had integrity. It wasn't her secret to tell.

"He went after the Densmore collapsed."

"To dry out. His partner probably thought it was the only way to stop him from killing again."

"He didn't do it. He's innocent."

"He's a drunk or an addict. Either way, he was that way before the Densmore collapsed. That makes him guilty, and you knew it."

"I knew nothing of the kind."

"Your report is finished, Gabrielle. Ziko's drinking or addiction led to a design that failed. Criminal negligence at the most. Fraud and malfeasance at least. I'm turning in your report like that."

"You can't. It's not true."

"At eight oh five, it's done. At eight ten, you can have your resignation on my desk. You're through here."

"No." She needed that job or she and her mother would lose everything.

And all she had to do to prevent it was tell Christian's secret. Cal might not understand Christian's problem, he still might report it as the reason for the Densmore debacle. But he also might hesitate.

Need weighed against need. Time elongated. Still, her lips remained closed.

"I'll expect you in the office later to clean out your desk." Cal hung up.

Why hadn't she spoken? What did she owe that bastard Christian after the way he'd treated her over the phone? She'd wanted to hurt him and she'd had the opportunity. But she hadn't.

She was pathetic. Now she was unemployed. Throwing herself on the bed, she let the sobs overwhelm her, tearing from her throat like blood from a wound.

Gabrielle hadn't leaked the story. She hadn't withheld information from her report. Two false accusations had ripped her safe world apart. She was as much a turtle as she'd accused Christian of being. Her history was littered with the hurts men had dealt her. After each hurt, she'd pulled in her head and hid. She was hiding again, not living. Working sixty hours a week and only seeing her mother, not making friends. No, she wasn't living.

She and Christian were reflections of each other. Maybe that's why they felt like yin and yang together. They both needed to come out of their shells, but neither would without the other.

Maybe they no longer had a future together, but she could help him come out of his shell by proving she didn't call the press. Someone else had. Someone who'd dogged their every step since Christian had decided to investigate. That person had tried to stall Christian, impede his progress. Now, when Christian needed to be focused on the upcoming trial, he had to fend off reporters and their accusations. He'd waste his final day of freedom doing something other than investigating.

Someone else knew his secret. True, an aggressive reporter might be able to find the trail to Crittenden, but only if he or she was pointed that way. No, someone who knew the secret had spilled the beans. Christian's brother knew. So did his partner. Brittany might know; Gabrielle wouldn't put listening at keyholes past the secretary. Jeremy Barrett might have learned the secret the same way. The vision she'd gotten from touching his hand showed he'd learned something he wasn't meant to hear.

Christian's lawyer might know. And Christian's doctor, Sean Bergman, Paul and Roger's friend. But the lawyer and the doctor had no motive. The lawyer had recently come into Christian's life. She wasn't sure how long Sean had been treating Christian, but she doubted he'd tell the press.

That left four suspects, two of whose names cropped up again and again: Paul and Brittany. Someone Christian trusted was guilty. Someone who knew enough to separate Christian from Gabrielle, leaving Christian without backup. Leaving him vulnerable and alone.

My God, it was brilliant. How had someone known his point of vulnerability? Because someone had been following them for days. But she knew of only one suspect who had power over Christian.

She had to get to Christian.

CHAPTER 22

Christian pulled into the Densmore's parking lot barely able to see through the deluge of rain, which was good because he didn't want to see the ruin. In fact, he'd protested meeting Jeremy here, but Jeremy had said the West Park jobsite down the road was too crowded with workers waiting out the rain.

Jeremy's car was empty. For some reason, he must have gone inside the building. Christian took a deep breath and steeled himself to face his worst nightmare.

He ran the hundred feet to the Densmore's front door, where the chain dangled loosely from one handle. Inside, the lobby was dim because not all of the overhead lights were on. He smelled a faint odor of coffee, and then he located Jeremy in the center of the atrium.

Christian removed his raincoat, wiping water from his soaking face and hair. "I don't know why we had to meet inside."

Jeremy turned to him. "This is where it all began, this monument to your greatness." There was a bitter tone to his words. He took a sip from the Starbucks cup he held, and gestured to another cup on the girder that lay in the lobby. "Help yourself to some coffee. It's decaf. I know you don't drink caffeine." Again, there was an odd note to his words.

Christian made a mental note to talk to Roger about his son. Jeremy's breakup with his girlfriend had made the young man angry at the world. Christian laid his raincoat over the girder and sipped the fragrant coffee. It was heady and sweet, nectar of the gods. He sighed with relief. He hadn't thought to have breakfast or make coffee this morning. Not with Gabrielle's betrayal and her strange accusations absorbing all his energy. He drank half the cup while he watched Jeremy wander the lobby, studying the destruction with an absorbed horror on his face. Christian knew the feeling.

Finally Jeremy approached him. "You want my handwriting sample." There was accusation in his tone. "My lawyer says I should give it to you so I won't be called to testify."

"We need it to rule out suspects."

"Suspects. Do you think I'm a suspect because I'm not a partner?"

"Roger gave us a sample."

Jeremy snorted. "I'd like to have seen that. Dad's golden boy accusing him of wrongdoing. I bet he's not so enamored with you now."

"Your dad's been under a lot of pressure lately."

"Yeah and now I know why. I read this morning's paper. I never would have thought you were a drug addict. Hell, you don't even drink caffeine."

As Christian took another swig, he refused to explain that caffeine didn't mix with his meds. Jeremy seemed too volatile right now. Besides, he'd never felt compelled to confide in his partner's son. He grabbed the plastic portfolio from the girder and removed a tablet from inside. The sooner he got out of here, the better.

"I brought paper for you to write on." He held the tablet out toward Jeremy.

Jeremy took it. "Of course you did. You're always so thorough." He looked around. "But not always."

Guilt stabbed through Christian again and he looked away. He didn't need reminders of how often he'd been a fool in the past months, not with this morning's disaster fresh in his mind.

"Yeah." He yawned, wishing for once he was allowed to have caffeine. He'd slept badly without Gabrielle and been woken by the press before he was ready to face the day. Behind him, the scratch of pen on paper meant he would be able to go back to his bed soon. Alone.

Another yawn caught him by surprise. Had he accidentally taken his medicine twice? Taken too many pain pills? He stared at the Starbucks cup and wondered how he was going to make it home before he fell asleep.

"I slipped a mickey in your cup." Jeremy said from right beside him. He caught the cup as it slipped from Christian's hand.

"A mickey? Why?" The edges of things were fuzzy, like when he'd been drugged at Crittenden.

"You should have stopped poking your nose in where it didn't belong. I thought the car accident would keep you out of the way long enough for the trial to begin. But you went right back to snooping the next day. You and that psychic." The last word was sneered.

Christian's legs buckled and he collapsed against the girder. "You altered the drawing." Were his words slurred?

"Yeah. It was supposed to show my dad I was good enough to become a partner. But it didn't pass the test. It was such an easy fix, it should have passed DesignCorp's testing just like the first drawing did."

Anger tried to burn off the drug haze. This spoiled brat had killed innocent people in his stupidity about architecture. "The length mattered." It was a struggle to make his brain work, and even harder to make his mouth say the words. "Like a seesaw. Weight equalization."

Jeremy frowned. "Huh?" Then he waved that away. "Then I overheard Dad talking to your brother on the phone. He was going to begin interviewing for another partner, for what was supposed to be my position in the firm. He said you were swamped with work and there was no one in the firm he trusted to handle the extra work. I was there. He should have trusted me. I'm his son."

Motive, Gabrielle would say. "You forged the test." Christian's tongue felt thick.

"Yeah. Me and Brittany. She was pissed at Dad because he

wouldn't get a divorce so he could marry her. She thought offering him sex would get her a wedding ring. Stupid bitch. So when he refused, she wanted to strike back at him. First she tried blackmailing your brother after she screwed him on tape, but his wife found out and filed for divorce. When the Densmore test failed, forging the test results was a way for both of us to hurt him.

"It was easy enough to get the DesignCorp forms. Your friend Jake is such a sucker for big breasts. Brittany screwed him right on his desk. I didn't think the length mattered. How was I to know? I didn't think anyone would be hurt except Dad."

Jeremy came close enough to lean over him. "When this collapsed, I figured you'd drawn a poor design. I was glad you'd screwed up. Then, when you kept poking around, I knew it was the test. I can't let anyone know about the test."

He crouched next to Christian and something flashed in his hand as he lowered it. Christian frowned. What was it? As he watched, as though from a distance, Jeremy stroked downwards across Christian's left wrist.

Pain seared him like a brand and he yelled.

"I know the real reason you were at Crittenden. I overheard my dad talking about it. He never thinks to close his office door. He said you get depressed. You were in the psych ward. Well, now everyone will think you were depressed enough to kill yourself."

Christian watched the blood welling over his wrist. He'd seen this before somewhere, in a flash of vision as Gabrielle had touched him. It had been a premonition of his death.

Jeremy grabbed his other wrist. Christian had no strength to pull his hand away. As Jeremy raised the razor to slash, Christian's mind screamed that this couldn't be happening. He didn't want to die. He wanted to live so he could apologize to Gabrielle and tell her he loved her. If she could live with his bipolar, he could learn to live with her clairvoyance.

Gabrielle.

*

Gabrielle tracked Paul Ziko down at a job site in Hamtramck. He hadn't wanted her to know his location, but finally he'd given in. She figured he was luring her in by playing coy with the location. But she was one step ahead of him. She knew he was guilty.

The white trailer marked 'office' sat innocently in a sea of mud at the construction site. She gripped her tire iron in her cold hands as rain ran in rivulets down her face. For the first time, she wished she was licensed to carry a gun.

She expected to find Christian in the trailer, in God knew what condition. Throwing open the door, she stepped into the trailer, brandishing the tire iron.

Paul looked up from a pile of blueprints and his blue eyes flew wide. He glanced at the tire iron, stiffened and backed away from the table. "What the hell's going on?"

The door slammed shut behind her and Gabrielle jumped. "Where's Christian?"

"He's gone. He got his handwriting sample and left about five minutes ago." There was a bitter edge to his words. He was obviously still angry his brother doubted him.

Gabrielle wasn't certain. "I think you're lying."

Paul backed up even further, glancing now at her hands. "Don't even think about touching me."

Gabrielle advanced on him. She had a weapon he feared more than the tire iron.

"I said keep away. You've got no right to my private thoughts. That's an invasion of privacy."

"I do when it concerns the health and whereabouts of your brother." She stepped closer.

Paul was now cornered in the back of the trailer. His eyes looked wild. "You're not concerned with Kit's health, only about crucifying him for your employer. He said you kept it secret that you were psychic. He thought he trusted you, but you betrayed him."

"No, you betrayed him. His own brother. Where is he?" She reached toward him.

Paul strained away from her hand, his chest heaving as he breathed. "I'm the only one who cares about Kit. I love him. I'd never hurt him."

If Paul was guilty, he was the world's greatest actor. She believed what he was saying. She didn't know what he had to hide from her touch, but it wasn't Christian's whereabouts.

She decided to confide in him. "You're not the only one who cares about Christian. I love him, too."

His eyes opened even wider. His mouth worked, but no words came out. Finally, he sputtered, "But your employer…"

"Michigan Casualty fired me for not telling them about Crittenden. I thought you were the one who leaked the story to the press, so I thought Kit would be here. I need to know where he is."

"He said he was meeting Jeremy Barrett."

Of course. "Where?"

"I don't know where. That's where he was going next."

"It's Jeremy. He's going to hurt Christian. I need to know where they're at. Paul, I need to touch you."

He pressed harder into the wall behind him. "I don't know where they are. You won't learn anything by touching me."

"You're closest to Kit. If something happens to him, it will affect you. If I touch you, I may be able to get a picture of the future and learn what happens today. Then I can stop it from happening." She hoped. It sounded logical, but in practice…No, today it had to happen exactly as she'd said it would.

"You can predict the future?" Paul said in an awed tone.

"Sometimes. Often, when Kit is involved. You see, he's the

other half of me. If he could accept what I am, there could be a future for us together. But I need to know where he is now."

Paul studied her, his eyes showing less white with every second that passed. Finally, he reached out his hand to her.

Gabrielle grasped it, like a lifeline. She poured all her hopes and dreams into her hold. Even if she couldn't have a life with Christian, she wanted him to live and be free of the taint of the Densmore.

The vision came with the sharpness of precognition. *Paul was dressed in black. Mourners congregated around him in small, murmuring groups. Bryce Gannon stood nearby, and there was Sean Bergman.*

Roger slid an arm around Paul's shoulders. "I should have listened to you. I should have insisted he go back to Crittenden. I believed him when he said he wasn't suicidal."

"So did I."

"I'm glad the city is razing the Densmore. I couldn't look at it again knowing Kit killed himself there," Roger said.

Gabrielle wrenched herself away from the grief and pain of the vision. Her throat was clogged with trapped sobs. Christian. "The Densmore." She sprinted for the door.

Paul yelled, "What?"

"Jeremy's going to kill him and make it look like suicide."

As she threw open the trailer door, rain slashed at her face. Bring it on. She still gripped the tire iron she'd forgotten she held. Now she was glad she still had it. She'd use it on Jeremy if he thought he could hurt Christian.

Kit. I'm coming.

*

Jeremy grunted and his hand jerked sideways, away from Christian's arm. The razor hit the floor with a clink. Jeremy tumbled backward away from Christian. A loud boom reverberated around the lobby. Christian wondered what was happening. Was the rest of the building collapsing? It was so hard to think.

Slowly Christian dragged his gaze to the door. There stood someone he least expected. Wes Masterson. With a gun.

"You killed my sister." Wes's voice quivered with deep emotion.

He held the gun leveled on Jeremy's chest. Jeremy clutched his shoulder, where a dark patch spread, and whimpered.

"No." Christian wasn't sure what he was protesting so feebly or why. Jeremy had just tried to kill him.

Wes glared at Jeremy. "You sick son of a bitch. You'd kill your dad's partner to cover up a crime. Your own boss."

"It was an accident!"

Wes shook his head. "I heard your confession. I know what you did. Now my sister's dead." His hand tightened on the trigger.

Wes was going to kill Jeremy. Angry, stupid, misguided Jeremy, who'd made a mistake and then compounded it with a criminal act. He needed to pay for what he'd done, but not with his life. Christian didn't care a whit for the sniveling, lying coward, but he cared about Roger enough not to want to see him grieve over his son's death. He'd grieve enough when his son went to prison.

And Christian loved Paul enough to know how much Roger's pain would hurt him. Friends shared one another's pain. He couldn't do that to Paul, not if he could stop it.

"No. Trial," he managed.

"Put the gun down, Wes." Gabrielle stepped into the lobby as her order echoed around the atrium. She stepped past Wes, who frowned.

Christian had never been so happy to see anyone, but he was afraid Wes would hurt her, either on purpose or with a wild shot. But he was unable to speak. She approached where he lay, then dropped to her knees and applied pressure to his wrist. Blood flowed scarlet over her fingers.

"He deserves to die." There was anguish and grief on Wes's face. "He killed my sister."

Paul stepped into the lobby, holding his cell phone out and open. "I've got 911 on the line. They're listening to this. Jeremy deserves to be punished, but not by you. You've suffered enough with your sister dying. You don't need to have his blood on your conscience. Let the court try him for his crimes."

"I want vengeance." It was almost a sob. "My sister needs justice."

"His father is my best friend, and I know he'd want him spared. So do I, for his father's sake. So does Christian."

Wes waved the gun wildly. "He was slitting Ziko's wrists. Doesn't that make you want to kill him?"

"Christian needs an ambulance. Will you hold us at gunpoint while he dies, too?"

Wes screamed his pain and frustration and rage. Then he slumped to his knees and began to cry. "Gina's dead. She's never coming back. She's dead."

Paul took the gun out of Wes's lax fingers. Christian was losing the fight with unconsciousness, but he knew one thing. Gabrielle had come to him. Even after the horrible accusations he'd made, she'd come to him. He owed her...something. Whatever it was grew foggy.

"Sorry," he thought he mumbled.

"Hold on, Kit, an ambulance is coming," she said.

And then he lost the fight.

CHAPTER 23

Christian swam up through the depths of a thick drug fog into the light of day. He thought at first he was at Crittenden, because of the hospital smell and the drugs, but the walls were the wrong color. Paul sat in a chair beside the bed, his head tilted against his shoulder, his eyes closed. Between the disarrayed hair and the dark circles under his eyes, his brother looked like hell.

"Paul." It came out a croak.

Paul's eyes snapped open. "Kit." He scrambled to his feet and reached for Christian's hand.

Only then did Christian notice the cast stretching from his fingertips to his elbow on his left hand. "What's this?"

"Do you remember what happened?" Paul's blue eyes were dark with remembered pain.

"Yeah. Jeremy tried to kill me."

"And almost succeeded." Paul took a deep breath. "He cut too deeply and severed a tendon, so you had to have surgery to repair it." He looked down and away. "I didn't know about the mickey Jeremy gave you. If I'd known, I would have made the hospital wait on the surgery."

Christian sensed something had happened, something that had scared Paul. "What aren't you telling me?"

Paul's blue eyes were filled with terror and remembered pain. "You nearly died of a sedative overdose, Kit. Between your regular meds, the mickey and the anesthesia, your system stopped. They had to do CPR during the surgery. I almost lost you."

Jesus. Christian swallowed. That explained the red plastic hospital bracelet on his right wrist that read No Sedatives. "Is there any permanent damage?"

"The doctors don't think so. The surgeon said your hand should be as good as new after some therapy. The hospital did an EKG on your heart and everything looks normal. But I think they're afraid of a lawsuit. Bryce shook them up when he was here with me the first night."

"First night? How long have I been here?"

"You've been in a coma for three days. We weren't sure when," Paul choked, "you would wake up."

Cold seized Christian's belly. His brother had been afraid Christian wouldn't wake up. As it was, he'd lost three whole days. "The trial was…" he couldn't think, "a couple of days ago."

Paul's face darkened. "You don't have to worry about that. Between Wes Masterson's testimony about what Jeremy said, and Jeremy and Brittany trying to blame each other, you were cleared."

"It's over?"

"Yeah. I saved the newspapers for you. Jeremy and Brittany were convicted, separately, of fraud and malfeasance. I think they must have had the fastest trials in Detroit history. Brittany forged the DesignCorp test results and Jeremy forged your signature on the drawing."

"Jeremy told me that part." It was too unbelievable and too unreal. He'd worked with both of them for a year and never suspected them. He didn't know how he could trust his own judgment again.

Yet Paul had come to his aid at the Densmore, despite his anger, and even Wes Masterson had protected him. And Gabrielle… she'd run to him despite how big an ass he'd been to her. She'd known he needed help, maybe through her psychic ability, the power he'd been afraid of.

He had to know about her. "Gabrielle?"

"I haven't seen her since the first day. I'd thought…well, she'd said she was in love with you."

Christian's chest swelled with joy and hope. "She did?"

"Yeah, when she was looking for you, the day this happened." Paul waved at Christian in the bed.

So Gabrielle loved him. But she didn't feel secure enough in her welcome to be here at the hospital. He'd done that to her. He'd thought he'd told her he was sorry at the Densmore, but maybe he'd only imagined saying it. He wanted desperately to see her so he could apologize, but there were things he had to say to Paul first.

"You can't keep trying to protect me anymore, Paul. I'm a grown man. It's time I stood on my own two feet and acted like a man."

"But your illness…"

"I'm not sick, Paul, I'm challenged, like a lot of other people. And those people lead full, productive lives without their loving brother having to smooth their way. I intend to be one of them from now on."

Paul's eyes were still concerned, but some of the tight strain faded from his face when he smiled. "My little brother's growing up."

Christian smiled too. "About time."

"So I guess Sean and I did the right thing by explaining to the press the real reason you'd been at Crittenden?"

For a moment, Christian cringed at the world knowing about him. Then his resolve firmed. His secret had kept him a prisoner. That wasn't what he wanted any more. "Yeah, it was the right thing to do."

"Then it's all right if I leave this place? When I thought… when I thought I might lose you, I didn't care if my business went belly-up. But since you're going to live and you don't need me anymore," his smile widened, "and the sun is shining for the first time this year, I'd like to check on my jobsites."

Paul had been willing to sacrifice his business for Christian. It was humbling and warming to be loved so much. "Have I told you I love you, bro?"

Paul clasped his good hand. "It's good to hear it now and again."

"How's Roger?"

Paul's smile dimmed and his blue eyes darkened. "He's holding up with Bryce and Sean's support. They've helped both of us. Good friends are as important as little brothers."

"I know that now. Would you do me a favor?

"Anything."

It was cowardly, but he was afraid Gabrielle might refuse his call. "Would you call Gabrielle and tell her I'm awake?"

Paul frowned, looking from the phone on the nightstand to Christian. "Sure."

Christian squeezed his brother's hand. "Don't worry about me, bro. But I'm glad you were here."

*

Christian stared out the hospital window at the first blue, cloudless sky he'd seen in months. His head was finally clear. There was only one thing missing now.

A sound at the door made him turn his head. His breath caught at the sight of Gabrielle dressed in a sleeveless blood red sweater and blue jeans. Even with her somber expression, he thought she was beautiful. His heart thundered in his chest. She'd come.

Her blue eyes were wary, yet concerned. "Paul called to tell me you were awake."

"Yeah." He wished she'd come closer. Her wariness hurt.

"It's my fault."

"What is?"

"Your coma. I didn't tell them about your...condition. It wasn't my place to say anything. At the time, I didn't think it mattered."

Something tightened in his chest. She'd stayed away because she'd thought he'd blame her. Again. He needed to apologize for hurting her. He took a deep breath and forged ahead. "It was my fault you didn't feel you could talk about it. I was an ass when I yelled at you. I hated having a secret like this, and being ashamed of it."

"Me, too. I think we've both been outed." She cocked her head. "I think you have some latent psychic ability. How do you feel about that?"

Blue eyes met blue. "I want to be normal, in every way."

"Me, too." There was so much yearning in her voice. An echo of a lifetime of pain and rejection for something she could not change. "I lost my job. My boss wanted me to tell him why you were at Crittenden, but I refused."

Something else to feel guilty about. "Barrett and Ziko Architectural needs a new assistant. You'd be an asset with your knowledge of construction."

"I wanted to be an architect, but I threw away my chance because a man rejected me. I was hurt for a long time after that."

Christian knew just how she felt. "I don't know if I can trust again, after Jeremy and Brittany."

"I know how you feel."

"You've always known and it's not because you're clairvoyant. I sensed the hurt in you."

"I sensed it in you too. It was like looking in the mirror. When's your birthday," she asked suddenly.

"June fourteenth."

She nodded as though she'd expected that answer. "Mine too. Gemini, the twins."

"Figurative, not literal, though. Two halves of the same whole. I knew it. If we could start again…"

She shook her head. "No."

Disappointment tightened his chest. He deserved it after the way he'd treated her.

Gabrielle came to his bedside. "No. Let's not start over. Let's go forward from here." She held out her hand.

Christian smiled and laid his good hand in hers. "Yes."

A vision filled his mind. *Gabrielle sat in a wooden rocking chair with her nightgown unbuttoned and one engorged breast exposed. She took the baby Christian handed her and the black-haired infant greedily latched onto her nipple and began to suckle. She brushed the silky head, a silver wedding ring glinting on her left hand as it moved. She looked up with love in her blue eyes to where he stood beside her chair. His left hand rose to cup her cheek, his own wedding ring catching the light.*

Gabrielle smiled. "The future looks good."

In the mood for more Crimson Romance? Check out *Finding Jordie* by H.J. Harley at *CrimsonRomance.com*.